JOSIE'S DREAM

PIONEER BRIDES OF THE OREGON TRAIL

INDIANA WAKE

FAIR HAVENS BOOKS WESTERN HISTORICAL ROMANCE

HARD TIMES ON THE TRAIL:

Planning your journey west was all important but no matter how careful you were things would go wrong and people would get ill.

The main problem was timing the journey. If you left too early in the year then the grass would not have grown. The grass along the route was needed to keep the oxen alive. They depended on it to travel the arduous journey pulling a heavy wagon. However, if you left the departure too late then winter could come before you reached your destination.

Often you see pictures of horses drawing the larger Conestoga wagons. These were too big to make the trail. The pioneers set off with a small covered wagon, usually a converted farm cart called a prairie schooner. They were named this because the white canvas coverings looked like sails from a distance. I can just imagine the sight of 100 wagons in the distance. The grass would look like a sand colored ocean and the wagons sailed peacefully on it.

These wagons were quite small, approximately 4 feet wide, 9 to 11 feet long and 2 feet deep.

Even with this size one of the difficulties was the oxen would become more and more tired the further you traveled and so you had to lighten the load.

Pioneers would leave all sorts of things along the trail. Discarded items such as crates, stoves, tools, blankets would all litter the trail. Those who lived at nearby forts would often follow the wagons and collect what they wanted.

I can just imagine this amazing trail dotted with belongings as the wagon's passed. Now imagine loading all your worldly goods into a prairie schooner and leaving for a five month journey. Now you have to lighten the load. What would you leave behind?

Josie's Dream is the third book I have written about women who travel the Oregon Trail looking for a new future. Each book is a complete story and they can be read in any order.

The first book was Trinity's Loss http://amzn.to/2xrn4B5

The second is Carrie's Trust http://amzn.to/2wGi86k

To receive two free Mail Order Bride Romance join Fair Havens Books exclusive newsletter. http://eepurl.com/bHou5D

God bless,

Indiana Wake

CHAPTER 1

*J*ohn Shepherd stretched his arms high above his head in an attempt to relieve the ache in his shoulders. He'd put in a long day, just as he did every day, constantly moving to stave off the chill of the cool spring air. Not only that, John was keen to stick to the promise he had made to the kind Townswomen of Oregon.

He was perfectly aware of how much he had to be grateful for, even in the midst of all his own sadness. Trinity Goodman, and a full complement of other ladies had arranged to care for his baby. Including Jeannie Stanton, and Carrie Easter. They had never once let him down and he was determined to return the favor.

Ever since Trinity set about assisting him and enlisting the help of others, John had been inundated with help as well as with food and clothes for his daughter. Far more than he and Leonora would have ever been able to afford.

Every morning, just as the sun appeared above the horizon, Jeannie arrived to take the first shift. Always striding in bright and happy, not a yawn nor a stretch in sight. She was a fine woman who seemed to adore baby Suki, and John could not help but think that she liked the early morning shift so that she could feed his daughter, and get her washed and dressed in something pretty.

Leonora would have liked her and would be at peace with the way Suki was cared for. As always, thoughts of Leonora stopped him in his tracks. John had been slowly coming to terms with the worst of all losses, and yet still, the emptiness had the ability to floor him without a moment's notice. Sighing deeply, he crossed the single room which had been home to him and his baby daughter since they had arrived. The last six months had flown by since the arduous deprivations of the Oregon Trail.

He peered down into the little crib and smiled when he saw Suki was still fast asleep, just as she had been when he had arrived back at their meager little home after a long day's work.

Jeannie had spent the entire day with Suki, as she always did on a Tuesday, and she had left him a warm stew on the stove. Hardly a day went by when one of the ladies didn't leave him something to tuck into when he came in from his farmlands, and he was always relieved and humbled by it. If he lived to be one-hundred-years-old, John didn't know how he would repay the Townswomen for their unerring kindness.

"John?"

He recognized Trinity's voice immediately; she always called out and then tapped on the door.

"Trinity, come in." John hurriedly opened the door and pulled it wide. "Suki is fast asleep," he said with a smile.

"She sure is a good sleeper. I reckon you have been real lucky with her, she is a wonderful baby," Trinity smiled at him before darting across the room to peer down into the crib, just as he had done moments before.

"I reckon she's asleep more than she's awake." John laughed. "But I will wake her gently in a little while and feed her before she goes down for the night. She is not just a sleepy baby, she is a real hungry one too."

"Well, I won't keep you, I can see you haven't eaten yet." She eyed the pan on the tiny stove. "I just wanted to see how long you reckon it will be before you move into your farmhouse. I might have some news for you."

"Oh, I see. Well, I reckon it won't be more than a couple weeks now. Dillon's help sure did make a difference, and I'm much further on than I thought I'd be. It's just a few finishing touches now and a bit of furniture and then me and Suki will be settling in." He smiled broadly, warmed as he always was by the thought of moving his baby girl out of the one-room lodgings they had been in for four months and into the home that he had been building.

John wondered what he would have done without Trinity and Dillon since he'd arrived in Oregon. Where Trinity had helped him with the care of his baby, Dillon had been equally helpful with the building of his farmhouse.

Fresh from his win of the bucking bronco's competition purse, Dillon had begun to build his merchant store immediately. He'd been able to pay several of the locals to help him out and, more than once, had sent them over for the day to help John get along with his own building. It was the sort of help that was invaluable and had moved things on for John very quickly. Without that help, it would have been several more months before he could have reached the current stage.

"I bet you can't wait," Trinity said with a smile as she looked around the little room.

"You have that right." He gave a laugh. "I reckon this room gets smaller and smaller by the day."

"You've done so well to get so far so quickly." Trinity stared off through the window. "Not only is your house all but ready, but Dillon tells me that you've already plowed up a couple of your fields and started growing. It won't be long before you're ready to start selling, will it?"

"In a few weeks, I'll be selling the first of the root vegetables, then the beans will follow. I turned a whole field over to wheat, so that should give me more income later in the summer." John smiled, proud of his achievements and excited by the thought that he would soon be selling.

"That's real good, John. And there isn't a person in town who could say you haven't worked for it, honey, because you sure have."

"Thanks, Trinity. It means a lot, but I couldn't have done it without all the help. I mean you, Dr. Carrie, not to mention Jeannie Stanton and Dillon. I was just thinking before you came this evening that I have no clue how I'll ever repay such kindness."

"You don't need to repay, John. It's enough for all of us to see you get on and it's not as if we haven't all received a little kindness along the way ourselves. I mean, if it hadn't been for Dillon and Carrie, me and Ma would never have got here, we would have just been stranded. And I'm sure that it's a tale that could be told again and again from just that one year on the Oregon Trail. And no doubt it will be told again and again come September or October when the next group arrives from Missouri."

"I guess so, but I'm still so grateful." He smiled. "Anyway, what's your news? You said you might have some news for me?"

"Oh yes, I was thinking about you today when I saw Josie Lane, do you know her?" Trinity raised her eyebrows expectantly.

"I can't say I do, but I guess I spend so much of my time out on the farm that the only people I see are you and Dillon and the ladies who come to look after Suki."

"Sure, of course," Trinity said and nodded. "Well, Josie Lane came across the Oregon Trail a year before we did. She is kind of young, just seventeen now, and she lost both of her parents along the way."

"That's real tough, did she have other family with her?" John asked, feeling the familiar pain of loss in the middle of his chest.

"No, it was just the three of them. The problem for Josie was that she didn't have any family back in Missouri either, no family at all."

"So, she just kept going?"

"There was nothing else for it. She was so far along the trail she would never have made it back by herself. But a family took her in, the Armstrongs."

"I can't say I've heard of them either."

"Well, they're setting up a farm just as you are, although they're getting on very nicely since they not only brought

5

their own equipment with them, but they drove Josie's family wagon the rest of the way also."

"So, Josie's family were going to set up a farm themselves, were they?"

"Yes, but Josie couldn't carry on alone. She was barely sixteen when she arrived in Oregon and the Armstrongs took her in. She's been keeping house for them, since they had money enough to get their place built in no time at all, and she also takes in laundry from the single men of the town and some of the better off families."

"She sounds like a hard worker. Poor kid," John said sadly.

"She is a hard worker, perhaps a little too hard." Trinity paused for a moment and chewed her bottom lip. "The thing is, she works for almost nothing."

"What do you mean?"

"She keeps house for the Armstrongs and does little bits and pieces about the farm. But her laundry money, every penny of it, she has to pay to the Armstrongs also. They say it is for her keep, her bed and board."

"But surely keeping house, cooking and cleaning, I daresay, and little jobs about the farm would be enough for bed and board, wouldn't it?" John found himself distracted for the first time in a long time, as if there was some comfort in applying his sympathies to the problems of somebody other than himself.

"To be honest, that is exactly what I thought. She takes in a lot of laundry, she is working from morning till night. I just can't help thinking that she's trapped there. Unable to save or make any sort of life herself because every penny she earns goes to the Armstrongs." Trinity peered down into the crib once more as baby Suki began to stir. "I sure don't want to say anything bad about the Armstrongs because they got her here to Oregon and they're looking after her in their own way."

"Well, you can leave it to *me* to say something bad about them," John said, feeling somewhat annoyed for the young girl on her behalf. "Because they are taking advantage, no doubts of that."

"I'm glad you said it," Trinity smiled.

"It's one thing to take somebody in and help them and something else altogether if you're doing it to line your pockets. It sounds to me as if they've turned her into some kind of household servant without any rights or means to make a life for herself. If they take all her money, every penny she earns, then she can't make any choices, unless somebody marries her. And that kind of marriage for a girl of just seventeen is no good, is it?"

John thought back to his wedding to Leonora and how they too were only seventeen. However, that was very different, he'd met Leonora the year before. The attraction was instant and they were so in love that there was no thought of them making a mistake. Even as he'd walked up the aisle, John had no doubts, no regrets, and he knew that Leonora felt the same.

When she became pregnant with their first child at just eighteen, John knew that their world was complete. He'd never once considered how his happiness could turn to sorrow. He'd never assumed for one moment when his beloved wife had become pregnant, that he would end up raising their child alone. A groan formed in his throat as the loss came rolling back. Coughing, he fought it down and pulled his mind back to the present.

"Well, she could end up just as trapped, couldn't she? A young girl like that who needs a marriage to save her can tend to attract the wrong kind of man." Trinity nodded. "But let's not marry her off just yet," she laughed.

"You have a plan of some sort, Trinity, I can see it in your face." John raised his eyebrows, Trinity always had a plan.

"Well, I was just thinking that in a few weeks' time you might well be in a position to take Josie on, to care for Suki?"

It had always been John's plan to only rely on the kindness of the women of the town for as long as he absolutely needed to. He'd told them all from the very beginning that as soon as he had his house built and his farm up and running that he would employ a housekeeper, someone to live in who would look after Suki while he was out at work. Perhaps by taking on Josie he would be solving both of their problems.

"I think that sounds like a fine idea, Trinity. Why don't you speak to her about it and see what she thinks about moving away from the Armstrongs?"

"I sure was hoping you were going to say that," Trinity gave him a knowing smile.

CHAPTER 2

*A*fter two weeks of working in John Shepherd's brand-new farmhouse, Josie began to relax. However much Trinity had tried to convince her that John was a good man, and that he was not going to treat her the same way the Armstrong family had, Josie still had not allowed herself to believe it. All her life she'd had a dream. A little family, a good man, and a house. In many ways this was her dream. Even though she was working for John, she was still loving her new life. Maybe one day she would have her real dream come true but for now she was happy to work hard, and to save some money and to live as much of the dream as she could.

It was only after the first two weeks were over and she had been allowed to keep the money she had earned from her laundry work that she had finally come to believe she had landed on her feet at last.

When she had first been introduced to John, Josie had been quietly skeptical. Although still only seventeen years of age, the last two years had taught her much, and had made her a little wary of the people around her.

"And you're sure, Mr. Shepherd, that I can carry on with my laundry work? You wouldn't mind?" Even though Trinity had assured her, when she had first met John, Josie simply had to hear it from him.

"Of course you can. And there's plenty of room about the place for drying when the weather is not so good." John had an open, honest face and he smiled at her warmly. "I reckon you really are a hard worker, Josie." He looked at Trinity who nodded vigorously.

"Mr. Shepherd, I'm happy to work here for nothing more than my bed and board as long as I am allowed to keep my laundry money. I've worked very hard since I arrived in Oregon, Sir, and never seen a penny for it." Josie had rehearsed her little speech in advance, determined not to make the same mistake twice. "But I will keep your house real nice and clean, cook for you, and look after your baby as if she was my own." She finished with a smile.

"That sure is a good offer, Josie, but I'm going to have to decline." He smiled at her as he spoke but she felt her heart plummeting towards the pit of her stomach; she had obviously made a mistake in being so vehement with her terms.

"Right," she said in a flat tone.

"I don't expect you to work for me for nothing, Josie." He grinned, obviously realizing that she had thought the worst. "I will still pay properly for the work you do here and your laundry business is yours alone, so don't go thinking that I'll try and take money off you for that. I can't have somebody here keeping house and looking after my daughter and not pay them. Not everybody is like the Armstrongs."

"I see." Josie could hardly put a sentence together she was so surprised. "Well, thank you kindly, Mr. Shepherd." Her voice finished off a little wobbly as his kind words sank in.

"You're welcome. Now, I guess I ought to show you around the place, although it's brand-new and I'm still getting used to it myself." He grinned at her. "And its *John*, you don't have to worry about the *Mr. Shepherd* part."

Josie called him John from that moment onwards. As she began to settle in and realize that he was true to his word with regards to the terms of her employment, it would have seemed odd to her to call him *Mr. Shepherd* any longer. After all, he was only a little over two years older than she was, and she could still see the boyishness in his face, even when his deep cares seemed to cloud over him.

Yet, she still thought of him as very much older, with so much more life experience and even a baby of his own.

Josie and baby Suki hit it off straight away, she was just such a happy child who loved nothing better than to roll around on a rug, giggling and bending impossibly so that she might put her own toes in her mouth. She really was a cutie, chubby with a round face and pale blonde wisps of hair and bright blue eyes, just like her daddy.

Josie thought it so sad that Suki would never know her own ma. The pain of her own loss was still intense at times and yet, Josie could not help but think that at least she had memories. She could remember her mother and father so clearly, she could see them in fine detail every time she closed her eyes. Little Suki would have no memory at all of the mother who had died just an hour after giving birth to her.

Josie had made herself low with such thoughts, and decided to busy herself by checking the wonderfully white sheets she had out blowing on the line. They'd had several days of warm sunshine and spring was definitely soon going to have to make way for the summer. It was perfect drying weather, that was for sure.

Lifting Suki up from the soft rug on the floor of the kitchen, she hoisted the chubby baby onto her hip and made her way outside. The sheets were blowing backward and forward in the gentle breeze and, as she stood in front of them to check how dry they were, Suki squeaked and squealed every time the sheets blew towards her.

She held out her chubby little hands as if to catch the sheets and, as they dropped down again, she reached for them, gurgling and mumbling as if trying to speak to Josie.

"That looks like a fun game you have going there." John's voice behind her startled Josie and she spun around.

"John, I didn't hear you back there."

"I was just heading back down to pick up my lunch parcel. I forgot it this morning." He grinned at her, his young face always so handsome when he smiled.

"You left it on the table? Goodness, I didn't even notice. I would have brought it on up to you if I'd seen it. I'm so sorry."

"It's not your fault I can't keep my mind on the little things." He smiled and Suki squeaked and held her arms out towards him. "Come on then, come to your daddy for a minute."

As Josie put Suki into John's arms, she couldn't help but think what a fine daddy he was. He always had a smile for Suki, even when he came in exhausted from a long day out on his farm.

Although she had only been there a short time, Josie could see that John was a different man when he held his child. In those few moments, his cares seemed to melt away, taking with them his sadness. It was as if baby Suki had him convinced that nothing had changed and all was right with the world. How sad it was that a man so young had already lost so much.

"I'll run in and get your lunch for you," Josie said helpfully.

"No, I'll come in and eat in the kitchen. There's no sense in me going back out there just to sit down again and eat." He smiled and led the way back into the farmhouse.

Josie could see him look up at the building as he made his way in, a certain amount of pride and satisfaction in his hard work, she had no doubt. It certainly was a fine farmhouse, neatly constructed and painted in brilliant white. Maybe Josie would even go down to the store and buy some seeds of her own and create a little kitchen and flower garden if John would be happy for her to do so.

"I'll boil up some water and make you some coffee," Josie said, setting to work immediately as they had made their way inside.

"Thank you," he said, setting himself down at the wooden table with Suki still on his lap. He unwrapped the parcel of bread, butter, and cheese that Josie had made up for him early that morning. "You've worked real hard in here today, Josie, and it's only just midday." He looked towards her, but

Josie turned her attention to the pan on the stove for fear that he would see her blushing cheeks.

"I mean the house is as neat as a pin, Suki is all clean, dressed, and happy, you've got all sorts of sheets and what-have-you out on the line drying. I can smell that you have something in the stove cooking for dinner tonight already. I guess the Armstrongs sure are missing you." He laughed a little and raised his eyebrows.

"I don't think it's me they're missing." Josie laughed too. "I think it's just everything I used to do for them. But I shouldn't say nasty things about them, they helped me get here after all."

"There's nothing nasty about you, Josie, and helping you along the Oregon Trail doesn't give them the right to take advantage of you, have no doubt, Missy, they *were* taking advantage of you alright."

"I think I knew at the time they were, but I didn't know what to do about it. Now that I'm here, now that things are so different for me, I guess I'm a little angry about it at times. I really did work my fingers to the bone for them, even when we were still on the Oregon Trail. I mean, I still lead my daddy's wagon along on my own most of the time, coaxing the oxen to keep pulling. It was only when we hit water and mud that I needed help, but then other people needed help too and I gave it. That was just the way it was out there, wasn't it?"

"It sure was, I certainly couldn't have made it without help after Leonora died." He paused for a moment and Josie felt suddenly a little embarrassed. It was the first time he'd mentioned his wife to her. "I couldn't have continued to drive my wagon along without all the people who helped me out along the way. Especially the ladies, taking it in turns to cradle Suki and keep her fed and safe. But when I got here, none of them decided that they had a right to extract money and services from me just because they'd helped. Quite the opposite; they continued to help right up until you came here to work. I guess my experience was the opposite of yours." He smiled at her sadly.

"It sure does sound like it. I think I just struck unlucky. But I got here to Oregon and that's the main thing. There was nothing back in Missouri for me, no family that I could rely on, so I just had to carry on. I suppose I had it in my head that I would carry out my folk's plans, but I knew, really, that I couldn't. And I couldn't have got the land by myself, I couldn't have worked it, and made enough money to pay for the acreage after the fourteen months was up. I reckon I fetched the wagon and all the farming equipment the rest of the way for nothing."

"I take it that the Armstrongs have kept your family's farming equipment, wagon, and oxen?"

"Yes, they just kind of took them over. I suppose they thought that I had no use for them, which was true really."

"Except that you could have sold them and at least had some money."

"Yes, I suppose so." Josie shrugged before taking the boiling pan off the stove and setting out two mugs for coffee. "But what's done is done and I'm just grateful to have a new life now and a better chance for myself than I had just a few weeks ago. I guess what I'm trying to say is that I'm really grateful to you, John, for taking me on here."

"And I'm grateful you chose to come here, Josie. Not just because of how hard you work, but because you brighten the place up." He smiled at her broadly before tucking into another piece of bread and butter.

Josie smiled at him before turning her attention quickly back to the coffee. Her cheeks felt so warm now, she hardly knew what to make of his words.

CHAPTER 3

"*A*re you enjoying yourself?" Trinity asked, almost dancing on the spot in time to the music of the fiddlers and the clapping of the crowd.

"I sure am, Trinity," John said brightly, despite the fact that he wasn't so sure he was.

"I don't know that I'm convinced." Trinity gave him a knowing smile.

"I'm sorry, I guess it's just the first time I've been to something like this without Leonora. We never used to miss a barn dance back East, she just loved to dance."

"It's just going to take time is all, John. I hope we didn't do wrong dragging you out here tonight."

"Not at all. And you didn't need to drag me, I really did want to come out and have a drink and hear the music. I don't think I'll be doing any dancing, if you don't mind, I just want to get used to things. To stand on the sidelines and take it in."

"Don't you worry, I won't go dragging you to your feet and

insist you fling yourself about like those stiff old cowboys over there."

"Stiff old cowboys *and* your husband." John laughed and they both looked over to the dancing where Dillon was manfully throwing himself into things enthusiastically with Jeannie Stanton.

"He sure likes a good time." Trinity laughed. "And he's met his match in Jeannie. Don't let her age fool you, she can dance without stopping from one end of the evening to the other."

"She sure is tiring Dillon out." John laughed and relaxed. It was good to be in company and he felt himself settle into the night a little more.

He had been feeling low about the barn dance for days, feeling somehow like he would be betraying Leonora by going out and enjoying himself. In the end, it had been Josie who had convinced him to go out for the evening.

"I understand your feelings on the matter, John. Not all the way; I mean, I lost my parents, not a husband, but I think I still understand how you're feeling." Josie spoke cautiously, as if she feared offending him or upsetting him.

But John had been neither offended nor upset; it had been something of a relief to find someone who didn't shy away from talking about Leonora and his loss. Everyone else was so kind that he couldn't fault them for a minute, but they always talked *around* his loss, being practical and helpful, not to mention cheerful, at all times. There was something different about Josie and, even though she went about it so cautiously, she still said things which other people tended to shy away from. It gave him a chance to let it go just a little more each time while gradually, bit by bit, the pain eroded and the good memories came back.

"I can tell that you understand, Josie, and I can't imagine what you went through out there on the Oregon Trail. Only sixteen years old, and both your parents lost so close together. You must have been real scared."

"I sure was scared, and heartbroken." Josie nodded thoughtfully, her quiet wisdom belying her years. "But I reckon it's a very different heartbreak, isn't it, when you lose the person you love most in the world?" She looked up at him, her pretty face a little pink as if she was flustered.

"I guess so, but loss is loss. None of it is easy, now is it?" He raised his eyebrows as he smiled in the hope that she knew that it was more than empty words; he really did care.

"No, none of it is easy, but I don't think it could do you any harm to go to the barn dance. It's not like you need to worry about Suki, I'm here to look after her. And Trinity's real understanding; if you don't feel like it when you get there or you need to come away, I'm sure she'll make it easy for you. Maybe you should just go and see what happens. You might even enjoy yourself."

"I don't know, I guess that's the part I'm most worried about," John said, and then stopped, not knowing how to explain himself any further.

"Because you don't think you should enjoy yourself, because you think that you'd be disrespecting your wife's memory somehow?" Josie's voice was almost a whisper and John could see that she was having a hard time looking right at him.

For a moment, he almost laughed; she was such a sweet girl.

But he realized immediately how much it had taken for her to even say it, not to mention the fact that she was absolutely right.

"I guess I think I'd be betraying her somehow, you know?"

"Yes, I know." She nodded a little, her cheeks still a touch pink.

Josie really was a pretty young woman. She had chestnut hair which was thick and wavy and shone in the sunshine. Her eyes were a pale kind of green, and her ivory cheeks were always so quick to blush. In fact, she was just the sort of girl who would have caught his eye if he felt a little differently about life.

"But you would know your wife better than anybody, wouldn't you?" she went on, quite determined, as if she had something she needed him to understand. "What I mean is, from your own knowledge of Leonora, do you really think that she would feel betrayed by you trying to make a life yourself? Do you really think that she would prefer you never to have a moment's happiness again?"

"No, I know she wouldn't." John laughed sadly and looked down at his knees for a moment, blinking hard so that Josie wouldn't see the tears of emotion which had welled suddenly in his eyes. "She wasn't that kind of a woman at all. I guess it's just me, isn't it?"

"I'm sure it is," Josie said as she spooned mashed vegetables into Suki's mouth, expertly catching all the bits that his little girl blew out again. "But I reckon it's a normal thing to feel like that. It's more like guilt than anything else, guilt that you survived and she didn't. I feel that way about my ma and pa sometimes, like I shouldn't be in the world without them, as if it isn't fair that I made it and they didn't."

John could hardly believe what a comfort it was to hear the words of somebody who understood his feelings as if they were her own. Of course, in her own way, they were her own feelings. Josie had suffered as he had, albeit in a different way. He knew that her words weren't simply easy comfort, platitudes given to carelessly smooth over his pain. They were carefully considered words; words that she meant completely.

"Won't you come and join in the dancing, John?" A breathless and frighteningly pink Jeannie appeared from nowhere and dragged him clean out of his memory.

"Not tonight, Jeannie, but you sure do look as if you're enjoying yourself." John laughed amiably; he liked Jeannie a good deal.

"Well, you don't know what you're missing," she chuckled wickedly. "I'm running rings around Dillon Goodman out there."

"You sure are, Jeannie," Trinity said, her eyes wide with mirth. "But I can see he's doing his best to keep up with you."

"Why don't you join them? I'll be just fine, Trinity, I promise," John said, realizing that he was holding Trinity back from enjoying the evening as much as she might.

"Are you sure?" she said, looking hopeful.

"I'll be just fine right here. I'll take a seat on one of the hay bales and finish up my drink." He took her shoulders and began to push her towards the dancefloor. "Go on, get out of here." He laughed and Trinity shrieked as Jeannie grasped her hand and pulled her energetically towards the dancing.

John sat on the hay bale, grateful for a little peace for a while. It was nice to watch everybody enjoying themselves dancing without any pressure for him to do so himself. He felt as if he was involved, without actually having to take part, and began to relax a little more.

However, he'd been no more than five minutes on his solitary hay bale when he felt somebody sit down beside him. John looked sharply around to see a young woman of around his own age sitting so close to him that they were almost touching shoulders.

"Aren't you dancing tonight?" she asked in a bright and kind of forceful manner.

"No, maybe next time," John said as politely as he could manage.

The young woman was certainly pretty enough and really well-dressed, but there was something about her manner that he found a little too imposing.

"Then maybe I'll just sit this one out too," she said with a wide, bright smile as she stared into his eyes. "I'll keep you company."

"By all means," John said, although his tone clearly suggested otherwise.

"I'm Catherine Thornhill, by the way." She twisted a little on the hay bale as if determined to look into his face and to have him look into hers.

There was nothing else that he could do but respond, not wanting to be rude to the young woman. However, John was not at all comfortable with her presence, and even less so with her close proximity.

"Well, it sure is nice to meet you, Miss Thornhill. My name is John Shepherd." He nodded.

"Yes, I know that already." She smiled at him in a triumphant manner, as if having already found out a little something about him was somehow a point in her favor.

For his own part, John felt a little disturbed by it. He wasn't quite sure he liked the idea of being in conversation with somebody who knew more about him than he knew about her. Although he thought the name Thornhill was familiar, he couldn't quite place it.

"You're the farmer who has a little baby to care for, aren't you?" Again, her manner was so direct that John felt himself a little on the back foot.

"Yes, that's me."

"So, who's taking care of the baby tonight?" She went on, her tone almost demanding. It was true to say that John was not warming to the young lady. "Local women have been looking after her, haven't they?"

"Yes, they have been. But I have somebody who takes care of her all the time now, now that I have my farm up and running." John was beginning to feel a little annoyed.

"Oh yes, who?"

"Her name's Josie."

"Josie Lane? The one who used to live with the Armstrong family?" Catherine looked a little put out, almost as if John's choice of housekeeper didn't meet with her approval somehow.

"That's right," he said, his tone determinedly short. He couldn't help but feel she already knew the answer before she asked the question.

"Well, I'm sure if you're not happy with her you can just get somebody else." She shrugged and looked out towards the dancers for a moment.

"Well, I don't think I need to do that. I'm real happy with Josie." Realizing that his tone was a little snappy, he decided to change the subject. "So, are you here with your folks tonight?" he asked in what he hoped was a friendlier manner.

"Yes," she said and blew out a great breath as if she was bored. "But my daddy is deep in conversation with someone or other from the provisional government office. He's not bothered with what I do. He wouldn't even mind if I just danced with anyone at all." Again, she looked at him hopefully.

"Well, as I said, I'll be sitting this one out." He looked back out to the dancefloor and hoped she got the message he wasn't interested.

"Never mind, I'll sit with you."

John had never met anybody quite as determined as this young woman seemed to be, and he began to wish that she had never made her way over to sit with him in the first place. All that was left for him to do was to make polite conversation and hope that either Trinity or Dillon very quickly tired of the dancing.

CHAPTER 4

*J*osie peered down into the crib and could see that Suki was, once again, fast asleep. She was well fed and it was nearing bedtime for the baby. Josie decided to give her five more minutes and then take her away to bed for the night.

She would just read a few more pages of the book that John had lent her. It was a romance story, one she had become very involved in, and she had realized immediately that it was not John's book, but more than likely one of Leonora's.

The fact that John had lent it to her without a moment's hesitation was something that Josie found particularly touching, and she was careful to turn each page gently, determined not to make a mark on the little book.

She'd taken to reading in the evening when she had cleared away everything from dinner and had Suki cleaned, fed, and ready for bed. It was a time to relax and John, more often than not, spent the time in the big sitting room in his armchair with his feet up on a little stool as he too read. Josie wasn't sure what he read, she was just certain that it wasn't a romance novel like the one she was reading.

Josie had to admit to enjoying the pastime, always having been a keen reader, but never particularly having any books of her own. Now that she had a little money saved from her laundry work and a new inclination to spend her evenings reading stories, Josie decided that she would go to the little bookseller in the town and buy some more books of her own.

"You're really engrossed in that, I see," John said, making his way into the kitchen quietly. "Am I interrupting?"

"No, not at all." She closed the book gently and set it down carefully on the table. "Did you want something to drink? I could warm some milk."

"I don't want to interrupt you. I didn't really come out for a drink, I just wanted to talk for a while, I guess." He smiled and took the seat opposite her at the kitchen table.

"Well, I'll make some warm milk anyway and you can have it while you talk." Josie felt suddenly a little tongue-tied, and found herself wanting something to busy her hands.

"If it's no trouble, then thank you." John seemed perfectly at ease with himself and Josie wished that she was just a little older. "I see Suki's fast asleep again." He laughed.

"I reckon she must be just about the easiest baby in the world," Josie said and instinctively turned to look over towards the crib. She really did care for Suki, almost as if she were her very own baby. "And she's just the sweetest little thing."

"She looks just like her ma," John said, but not sadly as he usually did when speaking of his wife.

Josie filled the pan with milk. "That must be a comfort to you."

"It sure is. I mean I can see a little bit of me in Suki, especially the pale blonde hair. But her expressions, and her smile, that's all Leonora."

"Then Leonora must have been very beautiful."

"She sure was pretty," John said and seemed eager to keep speaking. "First time I saw her was at a barn dance when we were just sixteen. I reckon I just about tripped over my tongue trying to say the right thing to her and she just laughed at me."

"You must have been real nervous." Josie laughed.

"I'd never been more nervous than that, I can tell you. And when she laughed at me, I thought that was it. I couldn't think of anything to say, and there she was all pretty and giggling, and I just thought I'd better go. I remember looking at the door and wishing it was closer so I could run out through it and hide." John was really chuckling and Josie thought it was a lovely, warm laugh. "But just as I took my first step away, she reached out and tugged at my arm and pulled me back. I don't know, something about it gave me my confidence back and I don't think we had a quiet moment between us from that moment until..." He couldn't finish, and he didn't need to, Josie could hear the tremble in his voice.

"I'm so sorry," Josie said and turned to look at him.

"No, it helps to talk about her. I guess I haven't found anyone I'm comfortable to talk to like I am with you. I suppose you understand how I feel, and it makes a difference."

Josie wasn't sure she understood entirely. After all, she could hardly begin to imagine the elation of having a child born and then, just an hour later, the shock and heartbreak of seeing your childhood sweetheart die right there in front of you.

"I reckon sometimes you just need to say this stuff out loud to feel like you can cope with it better. That's how I feel, anyway." Josie turned to look back at the milk, seeing the first bubbles forming around the edge of the pan.

"You must really miss your parents," John said quietly.

"I sure do." She stirred the milk for fear that it would burn a little if she didn't. "Not a day goes by when I don't wish they were right here with me. I wish we had our little farm and that my daddy could use all the equipment that I watched him pack so carefully."

"I wish there was something I could say that would make you feel better. I'm not as good at this as you are. You always know the right thing to say," John spoke a little sheepishly and Josie thought she could suddenly imagine him as a sixteen-year-old boy tripping over his own words as he tried to speak to the pretty girl he'd had his eye on all night.

"You don't do so badly." Josie laughed. "It's just nice that you listen. I didn't really have that after Ma and Pa died. But I suppose you know that, you just had to keep moving."

Josie was taken irresistibly back to that awful day, the day that she buried her daddy. With her ma dead just the day before and her daddy too sick to even stand up at her graveside, the poor man had lasted just a few hours longer. And on the day that she buried him, hardly hearing the minister's words as he made his hurried service so that the wagon train could roll on again, she knew herself to be truly orphaned.

Josie was orphaned in every sense, with no aunts or uncles or cousins in the world to take care of her. Mr. and Mrs. Armstrong, a strong and thriving couple in their middle thirties with no children, immediately offered their assistance.

Josie had wished that they had offered their assistance just a day or two sooner, then she might have been able to make her parents more comfortable. As it was, it had been left to Josie to continue to drive the oxen, to keep their wagon with the rest of the train. Her ma and pa lay side-by-side in the space that was really only just big enough for one in the back of the wagon. Every time the wagon train slowed or stopped for a while, Josie raced to the back and spooned water into their dry mouths and mopped their brows. At only fifteen years, she knew little of cholera and its effects. She had assumed that they would soon rally, as they always had from little illnesses over the years.

When the wagon train had stopped and Josie had run to the back, as she had been doing for several days, to realize that her mother had died as she lay there beside her father it was the biggest shock of her life. And Josie's pa was so ill that he had not been conscious for long enough to know what had happened. Maybe that was a blessing?

Suddenly, that awful feeling hit her again, almost as fresh as it was on the day that it happened. It was the day that she had realized that her daddy was undoubtedly going to die as well, and that she would soon be alone in the world. And her pain at seeing her beloved, beautiful mother lifeless in the back of the wagon was almost like a physical blow.

"Josie?" John was suddenly on his feet and at her side, quickly taking the pan of milk that was burning and boiling over from the stove and setting it aside.

"Oh, I'm so sorry," Josie said, confused for a moment before she realized where she was and what had happened. "My mind was... I guess I was thinking..." The tears were rolling down her face and John was finally looking at her. He looked more concerned than she had ever seen him.

Without a word, he wrapped his arms around her and pulled her to him, holding her tightly. Josie could hardly believe how sad and desolate she felt, thinking the worst of her grieving must surely have been behind her some months before. That her grieving had come out of hiding and sideswiped her so cruelly was a great shock to her, and a horrible reminder of what she had lost.

Unable to stop herself, Josie began to sob, soaking the front of John's shirt with her desolate tears.

"I'm so sorry, I... I don't know what..." she tried to explain.

"You don't need to say anything, Josie. It's alright, I know, I understand."

In the end, Josie didn't know how long she had been standing there leaning against him, her face buried in the thick cotton of his shirt and his arms tightly around her. She just cried and cried until the tears stopped flowing and her breath began to return to normal.

As she began to recover, John took her hand and led her to the kitchen table, sitting her down in the chair that she had been sitting in comfortably reading, quite content, before he had come into the kitchen. He silently returned to the stove and set the pan on it again, with fresh milk.

Josie drifted off into a world of her own, only looking up when John placed the mug of hot milk down in front of her on the table.

"Thank you," she said and looked up at him shyly as he took his seat opposite her.

"You're welcome, and you'll be just fine." He smiled at her reassuringly.

"I don't know why it suddenly took me like that. It was as if I was back there on that day, the day when I found my ma dead and knew that my pa wasn't long for this world." Josie paused to clear her throat. "I think about them all the time, every day, but never like that. I always think of them alive and well and happy and I miss them and I'm sad. I suppose I never think about them and what happened afterward. I never think of the worst of days because I guess I'm scared to. But it just happened, it just crept up on me."

"I know exactly what you mean," John said and reached out across the table to lay a hand on hers. "If it's any consolation, there is many a time it's hit me and I've broken down as I'm pulling the oxen across the field with the plow." He laughed sadly.

"It just takes you, doesn't it?" Josie said as she gently touched the skin around her eyes, feeling how puffy and sore it was. "Just suddenly."

"It sure does. But it'll get better, I promise." He patted her hand. "I promise."

CHAPTER 5

"*N*ow don't you just look like the prettiest little baby I ever saw in my life?" Josie said as she squeezed Suki's cute round belly.

Josie had clearly had great fun sorting through the huge store of clothing that Suki had, the many outfits that the women of the town had donated.

In the end, Josie picked a pretty white dress with a lace trim and a little bonnet to match. There was a pink ribbon around the waist and the same ribbon around the short, puffy sleeves. Suki's chubby arms looked short and adorable as her hands constantly roamed for something to fix upon and John, just coming in from a couple of early hours work on the farm, reached out so that she could take his finger.

"She sure does look pretty, Josie." John reached out to take her from Josie's arms. "I never saw that little dress before, but she has so many. The women of the town have been so good to me in so many ways and within days of getting here, I had more tiny clothes than I knew what to do with."

"The good thing is, they've given you all shapes and sizes, so she's got plenty to grow into. That little dress is kind of big on her, but she looks so sweet." Josie smiled at Suki, and John stared into her caring eyes.

She never hurried when she was dealing with Suki, always giving her complete time and attention to the little baby. It was clear to John that Josie cared a good deal for his daughter, maybe even loved her. For a moment, he felt a little emotional; at least Suki would have a mother figure in her life, a woman who would love her and teach all the things she needed to know.

"I guess I better give her back to you, I don't want to get her dirty." John laughed and bundled Suki back into Josie's arms as he looked at his hands and realized that he was, indeed, a little dirty from his morning's work.

"It's alright, she's still clean." Josie gave the baby the once over and then settled her down on her hip, just as happy as before.

John thought Josie looked really pretty too. She was wearing a dress that he hadn't seen before, and he wondered if she'd bought some material and made it up new with some of the money that she'd been earning from her laundry work. Many a night she would be sewing, mending dresses, or shirts and trousers for him. Other times she would take old clothing and combine two of the smaller baby outfits to make one new bigger one. Whoever made the new dress, sure knew what they were doing.

The dress was blue and white, covered in tiny little flowers, and she had several bright white petticoats holding it out at the bottom. Her wavy chestnut hair was tied back neatly with a blue-ribbon and she looked as fresh as a new dawn.

Of course, John had always known that she was pretty, there was no denying it. But what he felt at that moment was something that he hadn't felt for a very long time and the sudden feeling took him by surprise.

"I... I... I guess I'd better go and clean up and get changed for church," John said, trying not to stutter. "Don't want us to be late now." He grinned and hurried past her, hoping that she hadn't realized why he had become suddenly tongue-tied.

The two of them had walked down to the little church. It had taken more than twenty minutes, but Josie had been determined to try out the little buggy that John had someone make for Suki. An elderly gentleman, a friend of Dillon Goodman, had woven a sturdy basket and made a frame for it with the most enormous wheels. Josie had wheeled it about here and there, around the farmhouse with an excited, squealing Suki sat perched in the middle of it. However, she wanted to know if it could put up with the rigors of a walk to town and back, so that she might take the baby out on a fine summer's day without having to use the little cart and the horse.

"It's nice and easy to push," Josie said, her eyes firmly on the little buggy as they made their way along. "Here, you want to try?"

She relinquished control of the buggy handles to John and he tried to concentrate on where he was going, despite the fact that Suki was sitting bolt upright, her chubby fist gripping the sides of the strong woven basket as she studied him intently.

"There's no need to look so worried, Suki. Daddy knows what he's doing," John said and laughed before veering off a little to the left. "Oh," he said, trying to bring the little buggy back on course.

"I'm not so sure that daddy *does* know what he's doing," Josie said, leaning against a neat, white painted wooden fence at the front of one of the large, smart houses on the main street through town.

John turned to look at her and could see that Josie was leaning forward a little, holding her hand to her side as she laughed heartily.

"Oh, now, I wasn't that bad." John raised his hands out to the sides.

The buggy began slowly rolling away from him down the slight hill towards town.

"John!" Josie squealed and ran past him, she grabbed the handle in desperation.

Josie had caught the buggy before it was a few feet away and Suki was squealing excitedly, waving her arms in the air as if she was enjoying herself thoroughly.

"Alright, maybe I *was* that bad," John said, and it was his turn to laugh heartily. "You sure can move fast, Josie Lane."

"It's just as well." Josie was seriously out of breath and beginning to laugh again. "I think it's fair to say that you need a bit more practice, John. But not today, that's already more excitement than I can stand."

On and off, Josie chuckled and shook her head, all the way to church and John felt a strange lightness of spirit. It was a beautiful, bright summer's day, and he felt like a normal man again. A man looking forward to the church service and the rest of the day where he could relax before starting his week's work all over again. Just for a little while, he didn't feel like a young widower with a child. He didn't feel like a bereaved man with a heavy heart; he felt like a young man with things to look forward to.

The church service went well, with Suki only interrupting twice, much to the amusement of the other churchgoers and the patience of the Minister.

As they were singing the second hymn, John had the strange feeling that he was being watched and surreptitiously looked over his hymnbook to check if his instinct was right. He was surprised to see that it was none other than Catherine Thornhill, and she was making no bones about the object of her interest. She was staring at him fully, and when he finally caught her eye, she was not at all embarrassed. She just smiled at him with her wide, pretty smile, and continued to sing, not taking her eyes from him for a minute.

John was no more enamored of her then than he had been at the barn dance. That she was staring at him so openly, seemed to mark her personality as rather a pushy one as far as he was concerned. And, as pretty as she was, there seemed to be something spoiled in her nature that he found most unattractive.

With nothing more than a faint nod, John looked back down at his hymnbook determinedly. After a few verses, when he dared to look up again, he could see that Catherine's attention had been taken from him altogether and was now planted squarely on Josie. However, she was not smiling at the young woman who seemed entirely unaware that she was being studied, rather she was scowling at her.

It was such an open look of dislike that John was unsettled by it. He was glad that Josie, holding a squirming Suki on her hip with one arm, her hymnbook in her other hand as she swayed from side to side, was far too preoccupied to notice. Josie was a nice girl, one who would never look at another the way that Catherine was glaring at her. He didn't want Josie to see such open animosity, especially when it was undoubtedly aimed in her direction.

Catherine's behavior had clouded his day a little and it rolled around his mind all the way home. However, as soon as they walked in the door to the kitchen, John could smell the wonderful aroma of meat slowly cooking, his stomach growled as if to say 'feed me now'.

Josie hurriedly went to her room to change out of her Sunday best before returning to the kitchen to continue preparing the meal. She hummed to herself a little as she worked, periodically looking over to the crib, where Suki's snoring came like the sound of a cat's heavy purring.

Once again, John was taken by the feeling that everything was going to be alright, that he had things to look forward to. He couldn't quite put his finger on why he had that feeling, but he knew for sure that he felt more carefree than he had done for a very long time. He was hungry and looking forward to a fine meal. Yet content to sit at the kitchen table, occasionally glancing at last week's newspaper and otherwise glancing at Josie as she worked.

His peace was disturbed by a sudden and loud knock at the kitchen door. Josie began to dry her hands on a cloth to answer the door, but John beat her to it.

"That's alright, Josie," he said with a smile and opened the door inwards to see Catherine Thornhill, still in her beautiful Sunday best, smiling at him.

"Miss Thornhill?" he said quizzically, and could see that Josie was craning her neck to see who was at the door.

"As you see me," she said in a light and somewhat haughty tone as she looked around him, clearly indicating that she expected to be invited in.

"Won't you please come in?" John said in as polite a tone as he could muster. "You must forgive us, we're getting ready to eat." It was all he could think of to shoo her away with, but she seemed not to notice or care.

"Oh, it looks like we at least have a few minutes while your maid finishes getting the vegetables done, doesn't it?" She gave a hard little smile and John couldn't help but think that the comment was meant entirely for Josie's sake.

"Josie isn't a maid," John said in a serious tone.

"Of course." She shrugged as if it hardly mattered and looked away from Josie in a dismissive fashion. "I just came out here to tell you about the town treasure hunt next week."

"Treasure hunt?" John said incredulously.

"Yes, we're having a town treasure hunt, just for fun. It's next Sunday afternoon after church. I do hope you'll be able to go."

"Well, we shall see," John said, not wanting to commit himself to anything.

"I'll be really sore if you don't go, John. After all, I've been organizing it for my daddy. He likes to get the town together whenever he can, he thinks it's very important."

John, of course, now knew the name Thornhill. After the barn dance, as he had made his way out to his cart with

Dillon and Trinity, Trinity had made him very well aware whose daughter Catherine was.

As much as John had been concentrating hard on building his farm and caring for his daughter, he'd heard enough gossip to know exactly who Bart Thornhill was and exactly how powerful he had become in a very short space of time. John had known of men like that in Missouri, men who always paved their own way with money when all else failed. John had absolutely no inclination whatsoever to join in the town treasure hunt.

"Well, we'll see what we can do," he said firmly.

"Well, just see that you do now. Otherwise, I might have to come up here and get you." Catherine twisted a little from side to side in what she obviously hoped was an appealing, almost seductive manner.

However, it didn't appeal to John and he had to stifle a laugh at her determination. Still, he knew he ought not to be mean to the girl, and to laugh would have been unkind.

From the corner of his eye, John could see that Josie was about to reach into the stove with a thick cloth and take out the heavy pot with the sizzling meat inside. Without hesitation, he strode across the room and gently took the cloth from her hand, lifting out the pot and setting it down on top of the stove for her.

"Thank you," Josie said, and he could see that she looked a little unsure of herself.

He remembered that he'd told her almost nothing of the barn dance he'd attended some weeks ago when he'd first encountered Catherine Thornhill. Still, it hadn't occurred to him to do so until that moment when he thought, suddenly, that Catherine's presence might require at least a little explanation.

"Well, *we* will no doubt see you at the treasure hunt," John said, decisively opening the door in the hope that Catherine would just go.

CHAPTER 6

"What are we actually looking for again?" Josie was entirely preoccupied with Suki, who'd been something of a handful all morning.

Suki had sung her way through the entirety of the church service, even when everybody else had stopped and the Minister was talking. Josie had bounced her, and tickled her, and quietly pleaded with her to be a good girl, all to no avail. However, far from being annoyed, Josie had found herself simply amused with Suki's spirited behavior. Still, she had been distracted, and still was when they had made their way with the rest of the town to the start of Bart Thornhill's glorious treasure hunt.

"A fruitcake, apparently," John said and winced, and she remembered that he was not particularly fond of fruitcake.

"Oh, lovely. I like fruitcake, my ma always made it," Josie said with a smile. "But how are we supposed to look for it? I've never been on a treasure hunt before."

"Apparently, we get a handful of clues and we have to work them out and go in search of this cake." He shrugged.

"Ah, it looks like Miss Thornhill is handing out pieces of paper. I guess the clues are on them." Josie struggled to appear nonchalant, all the while wishing that she could have just gone home after church with Suki.

There was something about Catherine Thornhill that Josie had never liked. From the moment that Josie arrived in Oregon, Catherine had seemed to take a dislike to her. The two of them had hardly spoken, and yet Catherine always seemed to look her over every time their paths crossed. And to see her standing in the doorway at the farmhouse had come as something of a shock.

Of all people in the town, Catherine Thornhill was one of the last people Josie expected to be standing there. She had, however, been far from surprised when Catherine had referred to her as *the maid*. She was a pampered, spoiled woman, who undoubtedly had a nasty streak. It was clear to Josie that Catherine had wanted to belittle her in front of John for reasons of her own.

"Ah, John, here you are." Catherine swayed over to where they stood and managed to expertly place herself between the two of them, her back to Josie. "Now, if you look real carefully at these clues, you'll see I put a little something extra on your paper. You'll find the cake in no time," Catherine spoke in low, purring tones and Josie, staring blindly at the woman's back, felt suddenly annoyed and had to stop herself angrily announcing that John didn't like fruitcake in the first place.

"Well, thank you. We'll see what we can do, won't we, Josie?"

As soon as John mentioned her name, Catherine turned to

look at Josie. Josie smiled awkwardly as Catherine regarded her with a look of the utmost contempt. It was the same look the woman had given her in church the previous week.

It had been easy enough to ignore then. Not realizing that John and Catherine were acquainted, Josie had simply thought that it was just one of the woman's customary spiteful looks. It hadn't bothered her then, although it certainly did bother her at that moment. It was more pointed than ever, and Josie was very well aware that Catherine had her eye on John.

And why wouldn't she? John was young and handsome, his bright blonde hair and his blue eyes in so tanned a face were undeniably attractive. He was tall, with the broad build of a natural farmer and a deep-voiced and competent air.

Before then, Josie had thought that the only thing keeping many of the young Townswomen from trying to catch his eye was the fact that they knew he was grieving. Obviously, a fact that didn't bother Catherine for a moment. A spoiled brat like her wouldn't have cared less that a young woman had died giving birth out on the Oregon Trail. As long as it didn't interfere with her plans, that is.

"Well, I sure do hope you win, John," Catherine said, turning her back to Josie once more before she reached out to touch John's arm. "I made the fruitcake myself."

John didn't say a word and Catherine, with a wide smile, turned and slowly walked away, swaying as she went.

"I can't make any sense of this," John said, shaking his head from side to side as he began to read the clues on the sheet of paper. With a shrug, he handed the sheet to Josie.

"You obviously didn't read the extra line at the bottom, John.

The line which tells you *exactly* where to go and look for the cake, see?" She held up the paper and pointed to Catherine's secret communication with her finger.

"Oh, I see what you mean. Now that I look at it, it is a bit obvious." John chuckled.

"John, I might just take Suki and sit in the churchyard for a little while. It's such a nice day and I think Suki is a little bit high-spirited at the moment for us to join in."

"I'm sure she'll be just fine. And anyway, I don't want to wander about on my own." John pulled a face and Josie laughed. "And it isn't just Suki's high spirits, is it?" He squinted at her and grinned.

"Well, no, not really." Josie could feel her cheeks turning a little pink and she didn't want John to think for a moment that she was jealous of the attention that Catherine was giving him. "Look, Catherine has never particularly been a friend of mine and it looks as if she likes me even less now. I saw her glaring at me in the church last week and she's made it very obvious today that she doesn't want me here. When she made her invite last week, I knew I wasn't included in it and I've got to say that I do feel kind of uncomfortable."

"Well, it's supposed to be a town thing, so Catherine Thornhill doesn't really get to choose who does or doesn't come, does she?"

"I suppose not, but I do still feel awkward."

"I wouldn't want you to feel awkward, Josie, but I don't want you pushed out either." He took a step toward her and laid his hand on her shoulder. "If I've got to go and find this horrible fruitcake, I want you to be there."

"Alright." Josie couldn't help but laugh at the look on his face. "But Catherine isn't going to like it."

"I don't care very much what Catherine likes," John said and shook his head from side to side. "She's kind of pushy."

"Yes, I guess so." Josie didn't want to say too much about Catherine and she certainly didn't want to appear to be jealous in any way.

If she was honest, she *was* a little jealous, even though John appeared not to be overly interested in Catherine's charms. Perhaps it was just the idea that John was truly free to marry anybody he liked and at any time he chose. While he hadn't seemed particularly drawn to anybody, Josie couldn't help but imagine it as a possibility for the future.

It was something that she hadn't dwelled upon a great deal, because to dwell on it would mean her coming to terms with the feelings that had begun to grow. Not only was John kind and honest, but he was also handsome and funny and had become most attractive to her of late. It was an attraction that she had tried to deny, had tried to ignore, but ever since Catherine had appeared at the house the week before, the truth of it was never far away.

"So, what do you say? Shall we go and look for this awful cake?" John said and reached out to take Suki from her.

"Yes, alright then. But I guess we'd better look as if we are really looking around. You don't want anybody to realize that you know exactly where the cake is." Josie shrugged.

"That would certainly put a kink in Catherine's plan, wouldn't it?" John chuckled.

"You'd probably get away with it, but she would certainly blame *the maid*." Josie raised her eyebrows.

"You know, I should have mentioned this before, but she should never have said that last week. She had no right to describe you as the maid."

"She just wanted to put me down, John, and that is why I'm not comfortable, you see?" Josie could feel her cheeks turning pink again. "She looks at me as being in her way, I'm sure of it."

"Well, Catherine has got a disappointment coming her way. She doesn't know me very well if she thinks that I'm ready for love again, that's for sure."

"Well, no, exactly." Josie felt her throat tighten uncomfortably.

"Although, I suppose I don't particularly want to make an enemy of the most powerful man in town. I guess I'll just have to let her down gently." John shrugged, entirely unaware of the effect his words had had on her.

Although Josie had been a little jealous, the idea that Catherine would be thwarted simply because John was not yet ready for love again did not bring her any comfort whatsoever. She had immediately dismissed Catherine from her mind and thought about herself and her own feelings. If John wasn't ready for love, Catherine Thornhill wouldn't be the only loser by it. He wouldn't love Josie either; he couldn't.

"Although she probably wouldn't take a subtle hint." John carried on talking happily as Josie blinked hard. "Well, I suppose I'll just take it as it comes. She's bound to lose interest sooner or later."

"Yes, I suppose," Josie said quietly.

"Right, let's go and pretend to look over there, shall we?" John grinned and Josie followed him.

CHAPTER 7

*J*ohn had just set down the plow on the furthest field from the farmhouse when he realized he had, once again, forgotten the food that Josie had made for his lunch. She'd even called out to him not to forget it in the moments before he left when she had been busy with Suki in the sitting room.

Suki was just starting to crawl and had soon developed a quick pace, which meant that most of their conversations took place with Josie in another room chasing after the speedy baby. Josie was fully occupied keeping Suki safe and stopping her from escaping the farmhouse, and it seemed to have distracted her from her low mood of the last days.

John knew that Catherine's casual treatment of Josie had affected her a great deal. Josie was a good person who would never dream of being spiteful to somebody else, and so he thought it probably hurt her all the worse to have somebody be spiteful to her. He could see no real reason for it at all, except that Catherine was likely jealous of Josie for some reason or other.

While Catherine had more dresses than any young woman in town, and all the time in the world to see to her golden curls, she still lacked something. It was a quality, more than anything else, and it was a quality that Josie had without even trying.

And as much as John had tried not to think about the quality, whatever it was, he'd found himself lost more and more in thoughts of Josie. It wasn't just that she was already proving herself to be a fine mother to his baby daughter, or even a hard worker who never seemed to stop and never seemed to tire. It was her determination to get on with life, to make the best of it, which drew him to her.

Just as he had lost everything, so had Josie. Except, she had lost absolutely everything, with not so much as a family member to her name.

When she had been taken in by the Armstrongs and treated so shabbily, still, she hadn't given up. Josie had simply moved on without any discernible bitterness about the cruel hand that life seemed to deal her time and time again. A dreadful family had cheated her out of her family's own belongings, her father's farming equipment, and God knows what else that was inside his wagon. Yet she had carried on, moving to his farmhouse and working hard without any obvious signs of suspicion.

The fact that he had received genuine help after all he had suffered on the Oregon Trail and she had, to all intents and purposes, received none, did not taint her view of the world. She did not feel herself a victim, and had not become cynical as another person might in her shoes. As far as John was concerned, there was something beautiful about that. With her shining chestnut hair and her round green eyes, there was something beautiful about her in a tangible sense too.

Everything about her beat the likes of Catherine Thornhill hands down, and he could not help but think that Catherine herself knew it, and was jealous of her. Perhaps she had known it all along, and that was why she had been less than friendly to the poor young orphan who had arrived in Oregon a year before he had. The more he learned about Catherine, the more he realized that there was nothing in her personality to recommend her.

Deciding to ride back down to the farmhouse and take his midday meal there, John began to unhook the oxen. He would let them have a wander about in the top field for a while, free from the bindings of the plow.

However, as he worked at freeing them, his eye was drawn across the field. He paused for a moment and squinted into the distance, seeing Josie walking towards him with Suki tied neatly against her body with a shawl.

As she walked towards him, unaware that she was being observed, the light summer breeze gently lifted her hair which hung loosely about her shoulders. John felt his breath catch in his throat. She truly was beautiful.

She held his packet of food by the string holding it together, swinging it absentmindedly to and fro as she went. She seemed altogether carefree and something about her demeanor lifted his spirits.

John paused for a moment, his head dropping a little as he thought of Leonora. In his heart, he knew that he did not think of her constantly as once he had done and he felt a stab of guilt on account of it. Even though he knew that Leonora would not have expected it of him, would not have wanted him to live a lonely life of sorrow. Still he couldn't shake that last swathe of doubt. He couldn't entirely rid himself of the guilt he felt every time he found his attention wandering to thoughts of Josie Lane.

"Look what we have here!" Josie called out loudly as she grew nearer, waving the food parcel about in the air.

"I was just about to come down to the house." John laughed as he pushed the oxen, now free, out to roam on the field. "I don't know why I just can't seem to keep my mind on things in the morning. I know that's not a good way for a farmer to be."

"Well, it's not the end of the world. And anyway, Suki wanted to come out into the sunshine for a while." She handed John the packet. "We've got all our laundry done and out on the line, haven't we Suki?" she said into Suki's ear as she began to untie her. "And then we pulled some weeds from our little garden."

"Sounds like you've had a busy morning."

"And then we had to get Suki washed before she took her muddy hands over to the nice clean white sheet on the line." Josie chuckled.

"I think I can picture it," he said and looked at Suki who was smiling so brightly and chuckling, he began to wonder if she understood what they were saying. "Have you been a good girl? Have you been helping?" he asked and reached out to stroke her chubby cheek. "Or have you been crawling across all the pretty flowers in the garden as fast as you can flatten them?"

"There have been a few casualties, it's true." Josie laughed and set Suki down on the grass. "And it looks like you've been real busy too. You've nearly got his whole area plowed up. Your back must be aching."

"I don't mind plowing." He shrugged. "I guess I drift off into my own thoughts and before I know it half the field is turned over nicely." He looked all about him and realized just how much he had done.

"Well, you must be ready for something to eat then." She smiled and turned to chase Suki who had covered a surprising amount of ground in no time at all.

"I'll just wash up a little in the stream before I start on these." He called out over his shoulder before making his way down a little bank to the stream which ran across the top end of his farmlands.

When he reached the stream, John stood on a flat rock which protruded from the water, a little island. He crouched down on his haunches and laid his hands flat in the cold water before rubbing them vigorously together to clean them up.

Hearing Suki chattering, he turned to see that Josie had carried her down to the water's edge. Suki was wriggling, keen to get down to the water.

"Oh, no, you don't, little baby. You're not splashing about in there and getting soaked to the skin." Josie laughed, and John, laughing also, stepped back off his rock and landed half in the water.

"Oh!" Josie said as he scampered back to his feet and splashed to the water's edge.

John looked down and could see that he had soaked the entire right leg of his trousers and a good deal of his shirt. "It's a hot day, the water is lovely." As he flapped the fabric of his shirt ineffectually back and forth, as if it would dry out instantly, he suddenly became aware of strangled laughter beside him.

John looked to see Josie, red in the face from trying to hold back her laughter, finally she gave in. She covered her mouth but her eyes were wide and shining with mirth and he could see that she was highly amused by his plight. He stared at her open-mouthed for a minute and, as she began to laugh heartily, Suki joined in. Of course, Suki had no idea what she was laughing at, she was just content to giggle along with Josie.

"Sorry, I'm sorry," Josie spoke through her fingers before clamping her hand tightly over her mouth again.

"You don't look very sorry," John said, stifling a little laughter of his own.

He could see that her shoulders were shaking with laughter and the more she tried to hold it in, the worse it got.

"It was just so funny, John. And you're soaked! I'm so sorry." And once again she set off laughing.

"I did mention how nice the water was, didn't I? How refreshing it is?

John crouched down by the water's edge and cupped his hands, filling them with the cold water of the stream. As soon as he turned to look at her, Josie realized what he was about to do and her mouth and eyes opened wide as he let loose the water and showered her and a squealing Suki before she could even move.

"John!" Josie squealed but laughed excitedly.

As John crouched down again to get another handful of water, Josie began to hurry along the flat, grassy bank of the stream away from him. Without a second thought, John gave chase, laughing as he went and hearing Josie squealing excitedly as she tried to escape.

John caught her in a heartbeat, turning her around to face him as she breathed hard, her laughter high-pitched and happy.

Once he had taken his hold of her, John hardly knew what to do next. Having caught her, he couldn't let go exactly, but he couldn't lift her off her feet and plunge her into the stream, especially since she was still carrying a wildly excited Suki in her arms.

Instead, he simply laughed as they both began to calm down, their excited breathing slowing to a more normal pace as they smiled and looked into each other's eyes. John still held her firmly, knowing that he ought really to let go of her. With her cheeks pink from the excitement and her green eyes wide, he wanted nothing more than to kiss her.

His breathing steadied, yet his heart seemed to be going even faster, John could not help but think back to the first time that he had kissed Leonora. Just two weeks after the barn dance where they had first met.

Josie had looked at him with wide eyes also, and for an awful moment, John didn't know what to do next.

He released his grip on her a little, and took a step back. He continued to smile at her, hoping to recapture something of the humor and innocence of just moments before. However, he could see in her eyes that she had sensed a change in him, had sensed that there was something wrong, and he could see that it had hurt her.

Suki, however, hadn't noticed a change, and continued to wriggle and yelp happily. Josie quickly turned her attention to Suki, clearly pleased to find some distraction that would break the firmness of the gaze between them.

"You know it's going to take me all afternoon to dry out," John said and laughed as he placed a hand flat on Josie's back and began to steer her back along the bank of the stream.

"It's a hot day, I'm sure you'll be just fine," Josie said, recovering well as John reached down to pick up the food parcel he'd left on the ground.

"Well, do you want to share these sandwiches with me?" he asked with a smile and, while she accepted, he could see the hurt still in those round green eyes.

CHAPTER 8

"This sure is nice pie, Josie," Jeannie Stanton said as she tucked into her second slice.

"Apricot is my favorite too, but mine never tastes like this." Trinity looked hopefully at the plate and Josie, picking up on her cue, hurriedly cut her another slice.

"You ladies do know how to flatter," Josie said and laughed.

Josie always enjoyed the mornings when either Trinity, Jeannie, or both, called in to see her. Jeannie had been finding it hard to be separated from baby Suki and Josie didn't mind at all that the older woman called in as often as she could.

Jeannie was always very helpful, happily keeping Suki entertained while Josie got her laundry work done, something which was becoming increasingly difficult now that Suki was mobile.

"It's all true, I swear it," Trinity said, through a mouthful of pie. "I could eat that whole plate full."

"I've got to say, when you bake like that, I can only think it's all your hard work that keeps you so slim, Josie Lane." Jeannie chuckled.

"I suppose it's all the sheets I wash." Josie laughed too, enjoying the company of her friends. "I mean, I do enough for several households a week."

"But do you really need to keep working so hard?" Trinity ventured.

"Well, as long as John doesn't mind, I guess I'll keep doing it. I've managed to save a good bit so far." Josie shrugged.

"What exactly is it that you're saving for?" Jeannie asked, pushing her empty plate towards the middle of the table and laying her hands on her rotund belly in satisfaction.

"I'm not really saving for anything, Jeannie," Josie said, and thought about it for a moment.

It was true, she really wasn't saving for anything in particular. She wasn't even truly saving for a rainy day, for her employment seemed secure enough. At least for the time being, at any rate.

"Then couldn't you just let the laundry side of it go? Just concentrate on Suki and take a little bit more time to relax?" Trinity said kindly.

"I guess it's kind of hard to explain, but when I first got here to Oregon, when I was living with the Armstrongs, I felt very trapped. Although I was working, I had no money of my own, I didn't even have most of the possessions I'd set off from Missouri with. The Armstrongs saw to that." Josie paused to order her thoughts. "The thing is, there was nothing I could do about it. I couldn't fight the awful feeling that I would be stuck with them for the rest of my life, working my fingers to the bone and having nothing to show for it. I suppose that is what the money I save is really for, to keep that feeling away. I have something of my own now and I have choices. If things didn't work out here, I wouldn't have to stay just because I needed food and a roof over my head. Does that make any sense?"

"It makes perfect sense," Jeannie said, and reached out to gently pat Josie's cheek.

The gesture was so tender and motherly that Josie felt a little overwhelmed. Jeannie Stanton certainly was a motherly figure, not only to Suki, but to Josie also.

"But why wouldn't things work out here? As far as I can see, you and John get along just dandy." Trinity's smile was a little mischievous.

"Oh yes, John's a real good employer, I couldn't have found better really." Josie knew there was uncertainty in her voice.

"Josie, you don't sound so sure." Trinity reached out and poured them all some more coffee from the pot in the middle of the kitchen table.

"Not at all, Trinity. John is a good and kind man and he's a fine daddy to Suki. He's a hard worker and a fair and considerate boss. I guess I couldn't ask for more than that."

"You forgot to mention how handsome he is," Trinity said, her mischievous smile still in play.

"Trinity!" Josie shrieked, feeling a little desperate.

She really didn't want to talk about John in such terms, especially since he had silently rejected her down by the stream just the week before. It had clouded her every moment ever since and she knew it. In fact, Josie had not slept well for days, running the whole thing over and over in her mind.

Josie had been absolutely certain that John had been about to kiss her. Things had certainly grown a little warmer between the two of them, nice and slowly. But when he chased her down by the bank of the little stream, Josie had never felt so excited. She knew he was about to catch her and take her in his arms, she just knew it. And when he had turned her around, their eyes fixing upon each other as they stood, almost trapped in time, each wondered what would happen next. She'd felt so sure he'd kiss her. But when he'd backed away, when he'd walked her back to the field and they'd sat down to eat the sandwiches, Josie had to use all her determination to keep a normal countenance when all she really wanted to do was cry.

"What?" Trinity complained. "The two of you just look so good together. In fact, the three of you look so good together."

"Yes, the last time I saw you in church, you looked like the most adorable little family," Jeannie chipped in and Josie felt as if the two women had her in a pincer movement.

"No, really," Josie said, wishing they would change the subject.

"You're not telling me you don't find him attractive," Trinity persisted.

"Trinity, it doesn't matter how attractive I find him, he doesn't see me that way," Josie said, and silence fell in the kitchen for a few moments.

"I don't think you can be so sure of that, not really." Jeannie was the first to speak. "There's a kind of closeness between you, I've seen it. Everything is nice and easy, like you're both content and comfortable in each other's company."

"We are, but I suppose it's just because of our experiences so far. You know, the things we have both lost and the struggles and what-have-you. We have things in common, that's for sure, but other than that, John is not at all interested in me."

"Maybe he just needs a little time." Trinity had recovered and re-joined the conversation. "He's still grieving, I guess."

"I thought he needed a little time too," Josie said sadly as she thought back just a few weeks to the treasure hunt when he'd said that he wasn't ready for love. "But I guess that's just not the case."

"What do you mean?" Jeannie leaned her elbows heavily on the table.

"I think he looks ready to settle on Catherine Thornhill." Josie could feel her cheeks burning with humiliation.

"Catherine Thornhill?" Trinity said, her mouth wide open. "No, that can't be right."

"Catherine isn't John's kind of woman, trust me," Jeannie said confidently.

"That's just what I thought, he even said as much himself. But he's changed his mind, I know it."

"How can you know it?" Jeannie spoke gently.

"Because just two days ago she called round again and he walked out with her," Josie's voice was tiny.

"What? After church?" Trinity spoke with caution.

Catherine Thornhill had, indeed, called around to the farmhouse on Sunday afternoon. She had left it a little later than her previous visit, obviously wanting to be sure that John's Sunday meal was out of the way before she arrived.

She looked just about as pretty as Josie had ever seen her, her golden hair pulled back a little around her face and fastened with pretty combs while it ran long, free, and wavy down her back. Her dress, a different one from the one she had worn in church, was in a pale dusky pink, a color which suited her creamy complexion perfectly.

"Miss Thornhill? What can I do for you?" John had asked, standing back a little as Catherine walked confidently into the farmhouse kitchen.

"I thought I would come to see you for one thing," she said with a coy smile. "And for another, I thought I would take baby Suki out for a little stroll in that adorable little buggy you had made for her."

"Oh, I see," John said and Josie couldn't discern his mood from his tone, it was so neutral.

"I thought it might give dear Josie here a chance to finish up clearing the dinner things and then maybe have a little rest for a change." Catherine had smiled broadly at Josie, although Josie could see right through it.

It was clear to her that Catherine was trying a different tactic altogether and being nice to her, albeit disingenuously, was all part of it. However, John seemed to brighten a little, as if he believed the change.

"Well, that sure is a nice idea, Miss Thornhill."

"Not at all. And you must call me *Catherine*." She gave another bright, easy smile, and Josie wanted to yell at the top of her voice.

She wanted to tell John that it was a trap, it was all a lie and Catherine was the same person who had marched into that same kitchen just weeks before and spitefully referred to her as the maid.

"Well, let me get the buggy outside for you," John said, smiling and friendly as he wheeled the little buggy outside.

Suki, who was sitting bolt upright in her crib smiling and twitching excitedly, called out to her daddy.

"Oh my, what an adorable baby." Catherine, ignoring Josie completely, strode across the kitchen and lifted Suki out of her crib. "That's it, you come to Catherine," she crooned and Josie felt a dull feeling in the pit of her stomach.

"Alright, the buggy is all ready for you, Catherine," John said, returning to the kitchen.

"Why, thank you so much, John." Catherine began to make her way outside. "Why don't you come along with us? We'll only be having a little walk, won't we Suki?"

"Erm… Sure, why not," John said and reached up to take his hat down from the top of the dresser. "I guess we won't be long, Josie." He gave her a bright smile before turning to follow Catherine out of the door.

When she'd finished her tale, Josie let out a great sigh and leaned back in her chair.

"I couldn't stay here if Catherine Thornhill became… Well, if John…"

"My dear girl, you have him married off to her already after nothing more than a simple walk," Jeannie said brightly.

"Jeannie, I know you mean well and you're trying to make me feel better, but I know what I saw. John changed his opinion of her there and then. He believed the nice and sweet act she put on for him, I know he did."

"I don't know about that. She's real pushy and it sounds to me as if John was just being polite," Trinity added.

"I don't think so," Josie said sadly. "You see, I've seen John put her off before. She came around weeks ago and he more or less sent her packing. But this time he was all smiles and eager to get out of the door. He's definitely changed his opinion of her, I know it."

What Josie truly meant, but couldn't say, was that she was certain that John had changed his opinion of *her* as well. Maybe he'd seen in her eyes just how far she'd fallen for him on that day down by the stream. And even if he didn't really think as much of Catherine as she feared, perhaps going out for a walk with the woman was his way of silently telling Josie that he didn't feel the same way about her as she did about him.

"Well, don't you go making any silly moves, Missy." Jeannie said, becoming bossy and motherly all at once. "You just let things lie for a while and see what happens, alright?"

"Yes, I promise," Josie said, not sure that it was a promise she would be able to keep.

CHAPTER 9

$\mathcal{L}$ ater that week, Josie was enjoying something of a quiet day. She'd got through all her laundry work the day before and had even delivered it all in the little cart that she used when she and Suki went into town.

She had been able to give her full attention to Suki, who'd had a wonderful morning crawling at high speed and playing every game that her heart desired. Now that the baby had worn herself out entirely, she was snoring loudly from her little crib in the corner of the kitchen.

Josie had made herself some coffee and sat at the kitchen table enjoying what would have been the silence if Suki didn't snore quite so loudly. Still, the baby's snoring was a comforting, wonderful sound, which made her feel content and sad all at once.

Ever since she had told Jeannie and Trinity about her fears for the future, Josie had been unable to think about anything else. Every minute she spent with Suki seemed to be more precious than ever and Josie knew it was because she secretly wondered how much longer the two of them would be together.

Although she knew it was extreme, Josie couldn't help but think the worst and imagine her life without John and Suki. She tortured herself with images of herself standing alone in the church on Sundays looking across the pews towards where John and his new wife, Catherine, stood happily, Catherine cradling the baby that Josie had come to think of as her very own. The very thought of it brought tears to her eyes and, by the time Catherine Thornhill herself came knocking at the door, Josie was already in a very low state.

"John isn't here," Josie said gruffly as she stood in the doorway glaring at Catherine.

"I know he isn't, my dear girl," Catherine said in the haughtiest manner imaginable as she confidently pushed past Josie and strode into the kitchen. "I have just come down from the farm, so I know exactly where he is."

"Then why are you here, Catherine?"

"I think you'll find it's *Miss Thornhill* to you, Josie."

"Then you can address me as *Miss Lane*," Josie said angrily.

"Miss Lane?" Catherine said and threw her head back and laughed loudly. "Really, the maids at my house aren't as forward as you."

"I'm not a maid," Josie said, feeling her cheeks turn pink with anger and humiliation.

"Then what *are* you, exactly?" Catherine smirked at her and Josie knew the spiteful woman was enjoying herself thoroughly.

"Well, I'm... I'm..." Josie really didn't know what to say.

"I suppose you're the housekeeper, if anything," Catherine said as she took a seat at the table. "What do you think?"

"I think I'd like you to leave."

"Are you ordering me out?" Catherine said and laughed again. "But you're not the mistress of the house, are you? I don't really think you are in a position to order me out of the house, do you?"

"Then I'll go and get John and he can order you out." Josie was shaking with anger.

"Alright, you do just that." Catherine looked at her with a knowing smile and Josie feared the worst. "I'll wait right here with Suki and you can go and get John and we'll see what he has to say about it."

Josie stood rooted to the spot, not knowing what she ought to do next. She had the awful feeling that Catherine knew exactly how things would go if Josie rushed out onto the farmlands to find John and beg that he remove the unwanted visitor from the house.

Catherine obviously knew his feelings a little better than Josie did and she had the horrible feeling that if she *did* fetch John down to the house, things would end badly.

"You don't know what to do, do you?" Catherine's pretty face was marred by an ugly sneer. "Maybe you have realized finally that John isn't going to miraculously fall in love with you. I understand why you would encourage yourself with such a fairy-tale, but that's all it is, a fairy-tale, something that will never come true."

"You don't know me, Catherine. You don't know the first

65

thing about me or what my feelings are on anything. You took against me the minute I arrived here in Oregon, and you never gave any sort of explanation. I'm long used to the spiteful looks you give me, I was used to them even before I came here to look after Suki. I don't know what it is that's wrong with you, and really I don't care."

"Brave little speech," Catherine said, but it was clear that Josie had rattled her somewhat with her words and had likely touched a raw nerve somewhere. "And you're right, I have never taken to you, why would I? I could see right through you the moment you arrived; a poor little girl who lost her parents but bravely carried on along the Oregon Trail only to be taken in by a family who took advantage. Poor little Josie, isn't she just *so sweet*? Doesn't she just work *so hard* and isn't she just *so pretty*?" Catherine had never looked more twisted and spiteful.

"That doesn't even make sense," Josie said angrily. "With everything that you have in your world, how could you be so jealous?"

"Jealous of you?" Catherine said and dramatically looked Josie up and down.

However, Josie wasn't fooled by it, she'd heard her words and she'd seen her anger and she knew that Catherine had seen her as some sort of threat all along. Of course, Josie couldn't have cared less. It gave her no comfort to finally realize Catherine's motivation. In the end, it would make no difference.

"Why would I be jealous of you? I pity you, my dear. I pity your low circumstances and your poor, tortured little heart."

"My heart is not tortured," Josie said firmly, although her cheeks blazed and gave her away.

"It's alright, it's nothing to be ashamed of." Catherine's smile became a little sweeter but Josie knew not to trust it. "John told me everything."

"What?" Josie said, her head suddenly spinning.

"That's right, he knows how you feel about him and it just has him churned up to know that he will never be able to feel the same way about you. I'm so sorry to be the one to tell you, but I thought you should know."

"He shouldn't have said anything to you," Josie said desperately.

"I know, but he was just so worried about it all." Catherine's tone had become almost friendly. "And he knows it isn't fair to let you go on hoping."

Josie felt dreadful, as if she had been suddenly pushed from the edge of a cliff and was falling through the air blindly, not knowing when the moment would come that she would crash to the earth, breaking into tiny pieces.

How could John have been so cruel as to tell Catherine all about it? Had he gone as far as telling her about the afternoon down by the stream? Had he told Catherine how Josie had looked into his eyes with the hope that he would kiss her at any moment?

"I can see you're upset, my dear. Why don't I keep an eye on Suki for a little while so that you can have a little laydown or go for a walk or something? You look so upset, really you do." Catherine rose from her seat and made to lay an arm about Josie's shoulder.

However, Josie was in no mood to be consoled by her and jerked sharply away.

"You're enjoying this," Josie said, turning to accuse Catherine.

"No, I think it's very sad." Catherine was turning on the charm again but Josie just shook her head angrily from side to side. "But really, if you can't learn to live with me, then I think it would be better if you looked for another position somewhere else in town. Perhaps you would be better to take the room somewhere and just carry on with your little laundry business. I'm sure there's plenty of laundry to be done back at my father's house. I could have a word with him, if you like?"

"I don't need anything from you," Josie said angrily.

"Well, perhaps a position somewhere then," Catherine said and began to airily inspect her fingernails. "Because if you cannot bear to be in the same room with me, then I'm not sure how you'll be able to stay here once John and I are… well, I'm sure I don't need to spell it out for you."

Josie's head was in a complete spin and she wanted nothing more than to be away from Catherine, and even John. Especially John, now that she knew he had betrayed her. It was one thing not to return her love, that was his every right, but it was quite another to tell her innermost feelings to somebody as spoiled and spiteful as Catherine Thornhill, even if John was too stupid to see through her.

"No, you don't need to spell it out," Josie walked out of the kitchen and toward her own room.

She knew she couldn't simply pack up everything she owned and carry it into town. Instead, she put just a few of her belongings on her bed before neatly rolling them into her thick shawl. She would come back for the rest some other time.

With the shawl tucked under her arm, she knew she could comfortably walk down to Trinity and Dillon Goodman's newly built house. She knew that Trinity would give her shelter for a few days until she had decided what she should do next.

"Oh dear, do you have somewhere to go?" Catherine said with mock concern as Josie made her way back to the kitchen.

"Whether I do or I don't is none of your business," Josie said before crossing the room to look down into the crib.

Suki, the baby who could sleep through thunderstorms and the noisiest early morning calls of the cockerel, had managed to sleep through the entire argument. She was still snoring, her chubby pink face so sweet and serene.

As Josie looked down into the crib at the baby she had come to think of as her own, had come to love as much as she would have loved any child she herself had given birth to, she felt as if her heart would break. Perhaps John didn't love her and never would, but she knew that Suki did and she felt the sudden pain of loss that she hadn't felt since her mother and father had died.

"Well, don't you worry about Suki now," Catherine said brightly. "John knows I'm here and I'll wait right here with her until he gets back. She'll be just fine."

Josie blinked hard at the tears in her eyes, determined that they should not fall in Catherine's presence. The woman had won and there was absolutely nothing she could do about it, but she could, at least, walk out of that house with her head high and her dignity intact. She would not fall apart in front of Catherine Thornhill and, when the time came to collect the rest of her things, Josie was determined that she would not fall apart in front of John Shepherd either.

He'd made his choice and how he managed from that moment onward was none of Josie's concern.

CHAPTER 10

*B*y the time John made it to Trinity and Dillon Goodman's home, night was beginning to fall.

Josie had been there since late afternoon and, despite Trinity's best efforts, she had refused to return to the farmhouse to speak to John about everything that Catherine had said.

"Josie, I just don't trust it. Catherine Thornhill is a spoiled girl and I wouldn't put it past her to have lied about the whole thing. Wouldn't you rather speak to John about it all?"

"No, I don't want to see him. I can't believe that he told Catherine things about me that I hadn't even told anybody else. I can't believe he could be so cruel."

"But honey, you don't really know that he has. Catherine, I'm sure, is making the whole thing up."

"Trinity, I'm just so worn out. Everything that Catherine said was so close to the truth that I can't see how else she would have found it out. And John has been quiet these last days, ever since we were down by the stream." Josie had told Trinity, finally, about the moment they had shared.

"There are all sorts of reasons why he could have been quiet these last few days. And there are all sorts of reasons why he held back at the last moment, Josie." Trinity seemed almost to be pleading with her. "He was the one who chased you along for fun anyway, wasn't he? It's not as if you chased him, was it? And so, he backed out at the last minute, he's only human."

"I know you're older than me, Trinity, and I'm sure you know so much more and understand so much more of life than I do, but it seemed so real. Catherine was so confident in everything that she said that she must know that she has John's backing. And she even suggested that they would soon be getting married. I couldn't stay there and work in that house with Catherine as John's wife."

"You truly are jumping the gun here," Trinity said kindly before taking her hand in hers. "But you have cried yourself into exhaustion here and it looks to me as if you haven't been sleeping properly. I said as much to Jeannie the other day when we came around, I knew there was something wrong."

"I've hardly slept since we were down by the stream. It just hurt so much." Josie felt truly exhausted.

"Why don't you come and have a laydown. I think you need to sleep for a while, you can't go on like this. I think your exhaustion is making things seem so much worse, but you're not going to be able to get to the bottom of it until you've had some sleep. Come on, I'll put you to bed for a while and bring you some hot milk."
Josie was so tired she could do no other than follow Trinity's instructions. She laid down on the big bed in the guest room

as Trinity laid a warm blanket over the top of her. As much as her mind was in a spin, Josie fell asleep almost immediately. Exhaustion finally had her in its grip and she gave into it.

When Trinity crept back into the room it was dark and Josie had absolutely no idea how long she'd been asleep. She sat up in something of a panic, wondering where she was for a moment before the awfulness came back to her.

However, now that she had slept, now that she was not quite so exhausted, Josie wondered if Trinity had been right. Had she read too much into everything that Catherine Thornhill had said?

"I'm sorry to wake you, honey, but John is here," Trinity said with a warm smile.

"He's here now?" Josie said, feeling confused, wondering how he had found her.

"He is, and he's real worried. I think he's had as confusing a day as you have with Catherine Thornhill. Just hear him out, Josie, just hear him out."

"Alright." Josie began to rise.

"No, just stay here, I'll send John in. You need your privacy." Trinity hurried out of the room and in no time at all John was making his way in.

"Josie," he said and hurried over to her, sitting down on the bed at her side. "What are you doing here? Why did you leave?"

"I think you know why, John," Josie said, not ready to let go of her theory just yet.

"Well, I know it has something to do with Catherine

Thornhill, but I can't imagine why you would leave Suki and me because of something that she said."

"She as good as told me that the two of you would be getting married soon and that I wouldn't be needed anymore. She said it would be best if I just found another position somewhere else." Even as she spoke, Josie realized how ridiculous it all sounded.

"She said what?" John's mouth fell open and his bright blue eyes were as round as saucers. "But Josie, you know my feelings about that woman. Why on earth would you think that I would marry her?"

"I suppose because you went out with her for a walk the other day."

"Because I went for a walk?" John looked at her incredulously.

"No, it's not just that. You're making it sound all very simple, as if it was just one thing. But it wasn't just one thing. There are all sorts of things which, when I put them together, made sense."

"I'm sorry, I didn't mean to make light of your feelings."

"Catherine said things that she couldn't have known unless you told her."

"Such as?"

"Well, you must have told her about that day... you know, down by the stream." Josie looked down into her lap, her cheeks flaming as red as her hair.

"Josie, I have never told anybody about that. That is our

business and nobody else's and I most certainly wouldn't have told Catherine anything about it. Tell me, what *exactly* did she say?"

"She said that you knew how I felt about you but that you couldn't return it. You didn't feel the same." Josie's voice was low and she felt embarrassed and ashamed.

"And you thought that *that* was true? You thought because Catherine had said that that I must have told her about the two of us down by the stream? Josie, it never happened, I never spoke to her about it."

"I'm sorry, it just felt so real." Josie was beginning to feel foolish.

If only she had just thrown Catherine out of the house and waited to see what happened. Instead, she'd run away like a child and not only made a fool of herself, but had to admit to him how she really did feel. Things could not have been worse if she put her mind to making them so.

"You don't have to be sorry, Josie. Catherine is a meddler and she is a young woman who likes to get exactly what she wants. She's not used to people saying no to her, and when I did it obviously made her angry."

"You said no to her?" Josie said, a spark of hope rising in her chest.

"In a manner of speaking, yes," John said and edged a little closer to her. "I realize I shouldn't have gone out with her the other day for a walk. At the time, I really did think she was trying to be a little nicer, perhaps even apologizing for her behavior towards you. But that was it, I have absolutely no interest in her whatsoever." John bent his head forward a little, trying to make eye contact with Josie who was determinedly looking into her lap. "But as soon as we were out walking, I knew that she was trying to tempt me. I made it clear that I didn't have those sorts of feelings for her and, when she tried to suggest that I just needed a little bit of time to come to terms with my grief, I told her that I'd had all the time I needed. It was just that Catherine wasn't the one I wanted."

"I don't understand," Josie said, and finally lifted her head to look at him.

"It's true I've grieved, Lord knows I have. And who would know that better than you, Josie?" He reached out and took one of her hands in both of his own. "But it's time for me to move on and I realized that the other day down by the stream. But I panicked." He sighed loudly. "Forgive me for panicking, this is all new ground for me." He shrugged.

"What do you mean?" Josie wanted to hear him say everything plainly, she didn't want to make the same mistake again and assume his meaning.

"You've brightened my world so much, Josie. You've been kind and caring and you've listened to me and understood my pain."

"And you've understood mine."

"But I think we are both turning the corner now, walking out into the sunshine. I could feel it the other day when we were down by the stream. Everything felt so light and happy and I realized that I hadn't felt that way for a very long time. And yes, when I chased you and caught up with you, I wanted to kiss you more than anything in the world. And then I panicked, I had the same old feelings of guilt which have been holding me back from you for weeks and weeks now."

"I thought you were rejecting me," Josie said quietly. "I'm sorry, I just thought the worst. And when you went out for a walk with Catherine, I thought it was your way of telling me that we couldn't be together, that you didn't feel the same way. When Catherine said exactly that, I just believed it. I never felt so desperate in all my life, I just had to go. Oh, and it broke my heart to walk away from Suki." The tears began to roll down Josie's face. "Where is she now? She's not with Catherine, is she?"

"No, I wouldn't leave my little girl with Catherine Thornhill," he said and laughed. "I brought Suki with me, she's out in the sitting room with Trinity and Dillon."

"But Catherine was with her when you got home?"

"Yes, she'd made herself quite at home. She wouldn't tell me where you'd gone, just that you'd decided to leave. Well, I didn't believe that for a minute, and I sent her packing. I know that she realized when we were out walking the other day that it was you that I wanted and that's why she meddled like this."

"Trinity was right; I was too tired to think straight and I got this all so wrong." Josie still felt foolish but was determined to tell him everything. "And I'm young and don't know so much about this sort of thing. But I know what's in my own heart, even if I don't know what's in anybody else's. I know that I love you, John, so I'm just going to say it right out."

"That's all I need to hear. I love you too, Josie." John moved suddenly, scooping her into his arms and holding her tightly. "And I'm ready to marry you the minute you're ready to marry me. Come home, Josie. Come home and we'll be a family again."

"Oh, yes, I'll come home," Josie said, her eyes wide and bright with tears of emotion. "And I'll marry you."

Finally, John kissed her. He held her face gently in his hands and leaned in towards her, his warm lips wonderful against her own. Josie reached up and laced her arms about his neck, kissing him back with equal passion.

EPILOGUE

*O*nly Josie didn't go home. Trinity insisted that she stayed with them until the wedding. So, baby Suki and Josie spent a week in the Goodman's home being pampered by her friends until the wedding.

"I CAN HARDLY BELIEVE I'm a married woman already, and I'm not yet eighteen," Josie said as she and Trinity danced enthusiastically in the town barn.

The barn looked wonderful, decorated by Jeannie and Trinity with so many summer blooms that their fragrance seemed almost overpowering.

"Love comes when it comes, Josie. All we can do is just accept it and be grateful." Trinity swung Josie around the dancefloor until she shrieked. "And that man of yours sure does love you. I knew it all along."

"I guess I should have listened." Josie was breathless, enjoying every minute of her wedding day.

"No, you came to it on your own and that's always the best way. Now, come on, let's rescue your new husband before Jeannie Stanton finishes him off with that dancing. You don't want him tired out on today of all days!"

"Trinity!" Josie squeaked happily.

As she looked across the barn, Josie could see that Suki was happily being passed around between the many adoring ladies of the town who'd helped to look after her when she was so small. Then she looked at her husband, dancing for all he was worth to keep up with Jeannie Stanton. He grinned happily when he saw her approaching and Josie knew that she'd never been happier in her whole life. For a moment she wished her parents could have seen this day but she knew they would be happy for her. That they would be smiling down on her and proud of the new life she had found.

Before she knew it she was in John's arms and the whole world melted away as they floated across the dance floor.

"I love you, John Shepherd, you have made all my dreams come true."

He smiled down at her and she thought that she could melt in the love that radiated from him.

"I love you, Josie Shepard, more than I believed possible," he said and then he kissed her and the music died away until there was nothing but the glory of his lips on hers.

* * *

To find out when our next book is available join our exclusive newsletter and receive 2 FREE books http://amzn.to/2shQ9Ym

PREVIEW OF HOLLY'S CHOICE

This is my next book due out next week. I hope you enjoy this preview before it goes through final editing.

"I'm so glad you came today, Polly. Not just because I made more apple pie than I can eat, but because I thought you looked so downcast last time I saw you." Trinity Goodman smiled as she cut two immense slices from the as yet, untouched apple pie.

The two were sitting in Trinity Goodman's brand-new kitchen in her brand-new home. Her husband, Dillon, had made a good job of the place, building it immediately after he had his business up and running.

"I guess I've been down in the dumps for little while now. I'm just missing Travis, you know?" While this was true, Polly Whitaker knew that there was so much more to be said.

She wasn't giving Trinity the whole truth, and she knew it. Sure, she missed Travis; she missed him so badly it was like a physical pain in her chest. But there was more to it than simply waiting for him, much more.

"Have you heard anything this week?" Trinity had a really kind way about her to find out whatever she needed to, but Polly knew she was no gossip.

Trinity just cared, and that was all.

When Polly had bumped into Trinity in the grocery store just a few weeks before, she'd recognized her immediately from the wagon train. She remembered Trinity more from the early part of the arduous journey across the Oregon Trail. Anything after that seemed a blur, and whenever she tried to recall the details of the rest of the journey, all she could see was Travis Hurst.

As the two women had locked eyes in the grocery store, Trinity smiled broadly and called her by name. To Polly's shame, she couldn't remember Trinity's name at all, if she had ever known it in the first place.

Still, none of that had bothered Trinity, just as bright and friendly as ever. She had been instantly keen to find out how Polly had been doing, and had even asked about Travis. She seemed to know all about their sad, if temporary, parting. Polly found herself a little taken aback. Obviously, Trinity was a very much more observant person than she was. Not to mention the fact that she seemed to have a great capacity for caring for people, even if they were practically strangers.

"No, I haven't heard a thing from him," Polly said, the familiar sense of foreboding gripping her heart.

"Just nothing this week, or nothing at all?" Trinity spoke cautiously, obviously keen not to upset her.

"Nothing at all." Polly, had been about to raise a fork full of apple pie to her mouth, lowered it again and rested her fork on her plate.

"Are you alright, honey?" Trinity's face was that of concern and was absolutely genuine.

"Not really," Polly said truthfully. "But I'm real determined not to cry."

"You're with a friend now, Polly. You can cry all you want to, if that's how you feel. Don't you go holding back on my account." Trinity was so kind that Polly struggled to hold back her tears.

However, she reckoned she'd cried enough lately, albeit in the privacy of her own room, in the farmhouse that her father had built up so quickly when they had arrived in Oregon.

"That's so kind of you, Trinity. I wish I got know you better out there, out on the trail," Polly said, a little chagrined. "Instead of being wrapped up in my own world, Travis, and what have you."

"You were in love, that's all," Trinity said with a laugh. "And when it hits you, you can't always concentrate on everything else. To be honest, you were probably better off being in your own little world on that journey. At least when you look back, you'll remember the love and the dancing and the singing, and not the mud and the rivers and the Rocky Mountain pass." She finished with a warm smile.

"And yet now I wish I had something else to think about." Polly paused for a moment. "I'm sorry, I guess that sounds real selfish. Especially after everything that you went through out there, you must think me nothing more than a silly little lovelorn girl."

"I think nothing of the sort." Trinity tapped her plate with her fork and raised her eyebrows, indicating that her friend should eat her pie. "And I was all set to fall in love with Dillon out there on the trail before things went wrong. I know we got together in the end, but I would have been as lovelorn as you out there in the same circumstances. Don't be so hard on yourself, you're human."

"And I guess we can't change what's past, can we?"

"Would you really want to change any of it?" Trinity said gently.

"Maybe."

"Is there something you're not telling me about Travis?"

"There is." Polly's voice was so strained she hardly recognized it herself. "I guess I can't help thinking that Travis really isn't going to come for me." It felt so hard, so harsh, to hear the words out loud.

"And he's never written to you at all? I mean, you haven't had one letter in all the time that you've been here in Oregon?" Trinity reached out across the table and took Polly's hand.

"No." Polly felt a thickening in her throat and tried to swallow it down.

When she first arrived in Oregon with her mother and father, Polly had been sad, but also excited at the same time. In her heart, she had known that Travis Hurst, her first and only love, would be back for her soon.

All it would take was a little while, time enough to him to start earning money in the gold mines of California and get a place of his own. As soon as that was done, she knew that he would come for her. After all, that's what he'd promised.

Trinity had met Travis within days of setting off from Independence, Missouri, on the Oregon Trail. Travis didn't have much with him, no wagon, livestock, or farming equipment. It was just Travis on his horse with a laden pack carrying all his worldly possessions.

Trinity had spotted him almost immediately. He was so handsome and so big he could hardly be missed. Travis was tall and broad, the perfect build for a farmer or a rancher, and he had the lightest, sun kissed blonde hair and brown skin. His eyes were twinkly blue and his smile held just enough mischief to make him a little bit dangerous.

"Hey, you want to go up on my horse for a while?" Was the first thing he'd ever said to her.

The Whitaker family wagon was loaded to capacity and, unless somebody was feeling unwell, neither she nor her parents rode in the wagon during the day. They simply walked alongside, Clarence Whitaker, urging his oxen along while his wife and daughter kept him company on foot.

After the first couple of days, Angela Whitaker, Polly's mother, had realized that Polly would not disappear without trace if she simply wandered off and made friends along the way. And the very moment that Polly sensed her mother relax, she'd made a pretty good point of hanging back a little and giving an eye to the handsome young horseman who seemed to be watching her as much as she was watching him.

"But won't your legs get tired?" Polly had smiled at him.

"No, my legs be just fine. Here, let me help you up." Without waiting for her answer, he lifted her up onto the horse.

He lifted her so quickly and easily it was as if she weighed no more than a child. He was so strong, and Polly was instantly impressed, her mind already filling with romantic notions.

"My name's Travis Hurst," he said, lifting his broad brim hat just a little as he looked up at her. "What's yours?" By the way he smiled, Polly knew that he was as interested in her as she was in him, and the idea of it gave her butterflies in her stomach.

Now, when Polly thought of those first few days, it did not fortify her the way it had done when she first arrived in Oregon. Now it simply made her sad, reminding her of everything she had lost. Or at least everything she thought, and feared she had lost.

"Polly, did he actually say that he would write? I mean, some men aren't too good at that sort of thing, are they?" Trinity said, and Polly knew that she was trying to keep her spirits up.

"I appreciate that, Trinity." Polly smiled, feeling the warmth of her friend's care. "But it didn't need to be a long letter, did it? Just a few lines to let me know that he'd arrived in California safely and that he still loved me. That was all I needed really."

"I understand, and I am so sorry."

"I think I've been lying to myself for a good long while now. I haven't really allowed myself to imagine that Travis is never coming. Every day I go down to the mail office and ask if there's anything for me, any letters at all. And every day my heart sinks. I know now, even as I'm walking to the mail office, that there won't be anything. I know he won't have written. And yet, I still go. I can't let myself believe that it's all over." Polly's voice had levelled, and she was surprised that she had been able to speak the truth out loud without crying.

"Maybe he just hasn't been able to write to you for some reason," Trinity said thoughtfully. "He might have had an accident or hit some other misfortune."

"There were enough guys riding along with him to California who knew that I'd be waiting for him. I can't believe that something could have happened to Travis and not one of them would have got word to the mail office here in Oregon."

"I guess that makes sense." Trinity nodded slowly. "And it's comforting in its own way, I suppose. I mean, at least you know he's alright."

"Yes, if nothing else, I'm certain that he's alright."

"What do you think has happened?"

"Trinity, I can't help wondering if he's settled upon some girl down in California. Someone pretty or smarter than me."

"Now don't you go comparing yourself to some woman who probably doesn't even exist," Trinity said with a warm kind of sharpness. "Sure, you might wonder if he's found somebody else by now, that's only natural. But there's no need to run yourself down because of it, really there isn't. You're already smart and pretty, and you don't need to doubt that for a moment, alright?"

"That's kind of you, Trinity. I sure am glad that we bumped into one another in the grocery store when we did. I'm glad I got the chance to get to know you finally, and I don't know what I'd do without you now. I don't like to talk my fears over with my mama and daddy, they have enough to do. They've worked so hard to get the farm up and running that the last thing they need is to see me looking so downcast and feeling sorry for myself."

"Polly, I'm sure they wouldn't see it that way. I'm sure your mama already knows that you're feeling low and she's just waiting for you to say something."

"Yes, you're probably right."

"Look, why don't I give you something else to concentrate on for a little while?" Trinity said with a smile.

"But what?"

"I want you to come with me to the town barn dance next week. I think it would do you good to get out for a while and enjoy yourself, think about something else other than Travis Hurst." Trinity's smile had grown broader and broader. She was clearly looking forward to the barn dance herself. "Dillon is coming, but he usually finds somebody to get talking to, so we'd have time for dancing and gossiping. What do you say?"

"Alright," Polly said, nodding and slowly beginning to smile. "And maybe you're right, maybe it will lift me out of my own gloom for a little while. Thank you, Trinity."

Holly's Choice will be out next week to find out when join my newsletter here http://eepurl.com/bHou5D

PREVIEW 15 BRIDES OF THE WILD WEST

A 15 book box set with one brand new book, read on for a preview.

Jonny Peterson let out a long breath. He had finally arrived in Lincoln, and it felt like a blessing. An image of blood filled his mind, but he pushed it away with a shake of his head. The journey had been hair-raising, to say the least. When you had to run from home, the last thing you needed was to end up in the middle of a stagecoach robbery. There again, he guessed that was the last thing anyone needed!

Jonny picked up his suitcase, trying not to look at the bullet-ridden body of the man who had been in the carriage with him. Two cowboys loaded the body of Mr. Cormack onto a cart and covered it with a blanket. In Jonny's mind, they seemed too comfortable with the process. Maybe this town was rougher than he thought? It didn't matter, he would only stay as long as needed. Pulling his eyes away he thanked the Lord that it was not him and hurried out of the station.

A blast of wind hit him, he shuddered. It was colder than he had expected even for the time of year. Jonny shrugged against the wind and turned up his collar. walking away he ignored the growl from his stomach. It may want food, but Jonny had nothing on him, only a few coins in the money bag at his waist... it wasn't enough, he couldn't stop to look for food.

He needed to find the man he was seeking as soon as he could. That thought took away the hunger. It looked like he had been given an opportunity, it was one he would be sure not to miss. After what he had heard in the carriage, it seemed as if fate or the Lord had smiled on Jonny and he was determined to make the most of the situation. A wry smile crossed his lips the misfortune of his traveling companion could turn out most fortunate for him.

Picking up his pace he asked for directions and found the pastor's house on the same grounds as the church. It looked a little forlorn, standing at the edge of the cemetery. For a moment, he stood and stared, for the boneyard was densely populated with several white crosses. Too many of them looked new. Jonny tried not to look at them as he hurried on towards the house. A tall, thin man with jet-black hair cut short and real neat came loping out of the house. Almost skipping down the steps and making his way toward the church. Jonny quickened his pace.

"Pastor Philson?"

The man stopped and turned, giving him that pleasant look Jonny saw on many clergymen when they were meeting strangers.

"Yes? How many I help you?"

"I believe you're expecting me." Jonny mentally crossed his fingers. "I'm Jonny Cormack."

Pastor Philson's expression turned to one of recognition, his eyes widening.

"Mr. Cormack, of course, now please call me Phil or Pastor." He shook Jonny's hand firmly. "Glad you could get here."

"I nearly didn't. There was an attempted robbery on the way."

"I'm so sorry. Did you say attempted?"

"The driver and guard managed to get us away." Jonny's stomach twisted. "But not before my companion was killed."

Pastor Philson looked sympathetic and made the sign of the cross.

"It's such a shame. There is so much greed in the world that sometimes I despair."

Jonny silently agreed. His not so lucky companion had been full of greed and disdain for his fellow humans, especially women. Jonny hoped he wouldn't come across the same way.

Pastor Philson ushered him back towards his house.

"Would you like to come in? You look like you're ready to sit down."

"Please."

Jonny went gladly. He was ready to sit down and eat a meal; he hadn't eaten in three days and hadn't slept properly in four. Both of those were in the cards for him, depending on when he got finished with the pastor. The man had promised to help out, so Jonny was going to make sure that things were going to go smoothly.

Apparently, there was a lot of money in being a marriage agent. Jonny hoped it would be quick money. Right now he just needed to make sure things were going to go to plan and that he wouldn't get stuck in a situation he couldn't get out of. If his past caught up with him, he would need to run and fast. A little quick money would go a long way to help with that.

The two men entered the house, which was of simple tastes with a fire still going in the grate. Pastor Philson poured a drink, nearly filling the tumbler to the brim. Jonny raised his eyebrows and regarded this with amusement.

"I thought clergymen weren't allowed to drink."

"Technically, pastors are allowed." Philson grinned. "Besides, I don't drink. But it doesn't mean you can't. You look like you need it."

He handed the glass to Jonny, who took the drink gratefully. The whiskey burned its way down his throat, but that didn't stop him from downing it in one go. Wheezing as it melted his insides, Jonny settled back against the cushions. Suddenly he felt exhausted.

Philson sat on the other couch.

"So, when are the girls arriving?"

For a moment Jonny wondered what he was talking about. Then he remembered. The girls. The ten girls from an orphanage in Atlanta who were looking for love and new lives. His job, or more precisely it had been Jonny Cormack's job. For a moment he felt his stomach turn, but he had to put that behind him. What were the odds that two men who looked similar, had the same first name and could end up sat next to each other? When Cormack died, it seemed like fate and Jonny was more than happy to accept the job of marrying the ten women, with the help from Philson. Together they were to find each girl a husband and marry them as soon as possible. Then he would be paid for the marriage and Jonny could be on his way with cash to spare.

A hand went to his head, and he rubbed his brow. He needed as much money as he could make before he disappeared... and he needed it quickly.

"In three days." Jonny hoped his information was correct. He then remembered the letters and looked embarrassed. "Listen, I've been thinking. Some of the things I wrote regarding them may not have been appropriate. I want to apologize for that and ask for your help."

Philson smiled and shrugged.

"There's no need to apologize if you are truly sorry. However, it happens all the time. Men are desperate for wives and women are in short supply around these parts. Agents like you see a money-making scheme and you bring the girls here to be married off and pocket the fee. I don't like it, but it's not my place to judge." Philson chuckled and raised an eyebrow. "You're the first person who's apologized for it."

Jonny winced. He had no idea that marriage agents were this cruel. Only he wasn't a cruel man. Desperate maybe but not cruel and he wanted to make sure people knew that. Pastor Philson was the best person to start with on that score.

"Well, I know I said something about letting them fend for themselves once they get here. That was harsh." He shifted uncomfortably. "I shouldn't be leaving them to the wolves.

After all, they're meant to come here for a better life, not one that is worse, so I want to see that they are looked after."

"Did you hit your head on the way over here, Mr. Cormack? Because your approach right now is completely different to what you wrote to me before."

Jonny felt heat hit his cheeks and winced at the name Cormack. He must remember it was his name now if he wanted to pull this off. Cormack was dead, and he had left an opportunity for Jonny to earn some running money, only he didn't want to go into things too much. The more he talked about this, the more likely it was he would make a mistake. A smile crossed his face, if he had acted like this Jonny Cormack when his ma and sister were around, they would've paddled his butt, even though he was a grown man. To them that didn't matter as long as you were respectful of others.

Swiftly, he changed the subject.

"I know it's short notice but would you be able to help fix them up with accommodation? It's the least I can do. I haven't been able to do that myself yet as I don't know the area." He decided not to mention that he couldn't afford it.

"Of course not. My housekeeper's sister owns a boarding house. They'll have plenty of room." Philson tilted his head to one side. "Would you like the girls to have employment as well? Just in case they don't get married quickly."

"If that's possible. It will give them time to find the right man." Why had he just said that? The quicker they were married, the better.

Jonny hoped this wouldn't become a long-term investment. If he was lucky, he could get them all married off within a month, if not a couple of weeks. Then he could take what he was owed and leave. He couldn't afford to stay still for very long.

Philson was giving him a funny look.

"Are you sure you're the same Jonny Cormack who wrote letters to me about help getting the girls husbands and gleaning as much money as you can off them? I didn't like that man."

Jonny realized he had to be careful he didn't give himself away. The pastor came across as a nice, genial man who didn't suffer fools gladly.

"I'm the same man. Just had a change of heart." He swallowed and hoped he wouldn't get caught out. "Bereavement does that to you."

"I'm sorry." Philson's expression softened. "Who did you lose?"

"My brother." That was close enough, but Jonny wasn't going to go into it. "Will you help me, Pastor?"

"Of course." Nate stood and held out a hand. "Give me the names and everything you have on them. I'll see what I can do."

"That's all I could ask for."

Jonny fished out the documents from the satchel he carried and handed them over. The pastor disappeared into a room, Jonny guessed it was his study, and closed the door. Taking his glass, Jonny went over to the table where the whiskey was sitting and poured himself another drink. Then he looked to the skies.

"Jonny Cormack, you were one complete beast," he muttered under his breath. "Maybe these girls are lucky you're dead."

Find out if the ladies are better off in **15 Brides of the Wild West – A Brides Cowboys and Babies Box Set** now on SALE for a limited time at $0.99 or FREE ok Kindle Unlimited. Includes a brand new never before published romance.

MORE BOOKS BY INDIANA WAKE

To receive two free Mail Order Bride Romance join Fair Havens Books exclusive newsletter. http://eepurl.com/bHou5D

All Books are FREE on Kindle Unlimited

Newest Books

15 Brides of the Wild West – A Brides Cowboys and Babies Box Set

Trinity's Loss

Carrie's Trust

Hearts Head West

No Going Back

A Baby to Heal his Heart

For the Love of the Baby

A Father's Blessing

A Surprise Proposal

Mail Order Brides Out of Time

Blackmailed by the Rancher

For Love or Duty

The Baby and the Beast.

Saving the Twins

A Dream Come True

Box Sets

15 Brides of the Wild West – includes never before published book.

36 cowboys and Brides Mega Box Set with 5 never before published books.

22 Book Mega Box Set – 22 Brides Ride West for Love

22 Book Mega Box Set – 22 Frontier Brides – Love & Hope Ride West http://amzn.to/1Xf8xNR

16 Book Boxed Set Love & Hearts http://bit.ly/1kXbkw4

10 Frontier Brides and Babies 10 Book Mega Box Set

10 Book Box Set 10 Healing Hearts

7 Brides for 7 lonely Cowboys box set http://amzn.to/1SXaQVG

An English Rose in Texas 5 Book Set 2 books never before published http://amzn.to/1Tl64iH

The Mail Order Bride and the Marriage Agent Series:

The Mail Order Bride and the Stolen Baby

Secret's Lies and a New Family

The Right Choice

The Mail Order Bride and the Hunted Man

His Golden Angel

Mistaken Trust

Love at Eighty Yards

The Narrow Escape

2 Book Set – A Celebration of life & No Sympathy

Based on a True Story

2 Book Special Into the Unknown& Call of the Hunter

Novel Length books

Christmas Hope & Redemption

Strength from Within – Anabella

The Wrong Proposal – Evelyn

A Leaf on the Breeze - Amelia

Nancy and Claudine Love Will Find You

ABOUT THE AUTHOR

Indiana Wake was born in Denver Colorado where she learned to love the outdoors and horses. At the age of eleven, her parents moved to the United Kingdom to follow her father's career.

It was a strange and foreign new world and it took a while for her to settle down. Her mom raised horses and Indiana soon learned to ride. She would often escape on horseback imagining she was back in the Wild West. As well as horses, Indiana escaped into fiction and dreamed of all the friends she had left behind.

From an early age, she loved stories. They were always sweet and clean and more often than not, included horses, cowboys and most importantly of all a happy ever after. As she got older, she would often be found making up her own stories and would tell them to anyone who would listen.

As she grew up, she continued to write but marriage and a job stole some of her dreams. Then one day she was discussing with a friend at church, how hard it was to get sweet and clean fiction. Though very shy about her writing Indiana agreed to share one of her stories. That friend loved the story and suggested she publish it on kindle. Together they worked really hard and the rest, as they say, is history.

Indiana has had multiple number one bestsellers and now

makes her living from her writing. She believes she was truly blessed to be given this opportunity and thanks each and every one of her readers for making her dream come true.

Belle Fiffer is not your ordinary girl. She grew up in the west where she loved to ride horses and walk in the wilds. At fifteen, she moved to England when her father's job took him across the pond. Leaving behind all her friends she lost herself in books and if she is honest she fell in love with food. She is not ashamed of her curves and loves stories about good, honest men that love their women on the large side.

As a committed Christian, her books are clean, sweet and inspirational. Belle hopes you enjoy the books.

Made in United States
Troutdale, OR
06/11/2024

20475465R00072